This Kind of Man, a suite of dramatic monologues and meditations, seems to pick up where Raymond Carver left off: anatomizing all the ways that American masculinity finds itself adrift, with a special thought for the women in the same lifeboat. Murphy sees how we live so plainly and clearly that, in the best possible way, it hurts.

—**Louis Bayard**, author of *The Pale Blue Eye*

The stories in Sean Murphy's extraordinary collection *This Kind of Man* are swift, sharp, sometimes harsh, often sad, but so absolutely, transcendentally honest that the final effect is thrilling, a form of liberation. I know of no other eulogy for the post-war American male that so deftly captures the mingled love and anger of fathers and sons.

—**Robert Anthony Siegel**, author of *Criminals: My Family's Life on Both Sides of the Law*

In *This Kind of Man*, Sean Murphy excavates the complicated, tender, wild truth of what it is to be a man across generations and relationships. His wistful, funny, precise honesty lights up the page and helps the reader see the complexity of the filter of maleness. An insightful and necessary book.

—**Karen E. Bender**, author of *Refund*, Finalist 2015 National Book Award

With its refreshing vulnerability, frankness, and insights, *This Kind of Man* fills a void in our literary landscape by artfully capturing both the tender and tormented sides of masculinity. Sean Murphy's courageous stories do what groundbreaking literature should do—simultaneously comfort and disturb its readers. This is an important, indispensable read for our times.

—**Whitney Collins**, author of *Big Bad* and *Ricky & Other Love Stories*

Twenty-first-century manhood is a minefield – a terrain riddled with hidden dangers. A wrong word, a long-held grudge, even a mistimed joke can easily end in disaster. Traversing such explosive territory requires tremendous skill, a bucketful of courage, and no small amount of humor. Sean Murphy's *This Kind of Man* has all three, in spades.

—**David McGlynn**, author of *One Day You'll Thank Me: Lessons from an Unexpected Fatherhood*

This Kind of Man examines the moving target of modern masculinity and asks, from multiple angles, *What is a man?* The discourse around this question has been shockingly absent from the literary landscape, whether due to a lack of bravery or a certain paralysis that accompanies such an inquiry. Yet Murphy dives in head-first, offering stories that explore marriage, fatherhood, aggression, alcoholism, gender expectations, generational backlash, and more with nuance, humor, and an abundance of truth. His prose thrillingly invites us to think deeply. Instead of hiding from what it means to be a man today, he gives us a broad canvas from which to take in the answers, plural, to this essential question.

—**Cheryl Della Pietra**, author of *Gonzo Girl*

From yearnings never expressed by "strong and silent" types to competitive father/son relationships, veteran misogynists and burgeoning incels, Murphy's new collection looks straight at the worst traits of the white American male with a view to the future where these men can do better, be better, think beyond themselves. A timely, gripping read by a courageous writer.

—**Courtney Maum**, author of *The Year of the Horses*

THIS KIND OF **MAN**

Stories

SEAN **MURPHY**

THIS KIND OF MAN
Copyright © 2024 Sean Murphy
All Rights Reserved.
Published by Unsolicited Press.
First Edition.

No part of this book may be used or reproduced in any manner whatsoever without written permission except in the case of brief quotations embodied in critical articles or reviews. This is a work of fiction. Any resemble to real people is merely coincidence.

For information contact:
Unsolicited Press
Portland, Oregon
www.unsolicitedpress.com
orders@unsolicitedpress.com
619-354-8005

Interior Book Designer: Kathryn Gerhardt
Cover Designers: Sean Murphy and Morgan Ryan
Cover Image: Giuseppe Arcimboldo, "Fire," from Four Elements, 1566
Editor: Summer Stewart

ISBN: 978-1-956692-86-0

CONTENTS

I		13
	The Letter My Father Never Wrote Me	15
	This Kind of Man	18
	Winning	25
	Now's The Time	38
II		55
	Philippi	57
	That's Why God Made Men	77
	Red State Sewer Side	89
	Scars	100
	In My Cups	113
	No Tengo a Nadie	116
III		127
	A Brief Catalog of Mostly Forgivable Thoughts	129
	Life without Onions	133
	Later, That Same Morning	137
	How Many Men?	139
	Instinct	145
	Unbroken Things	154
	Our Vietnam	173
IV		183

Still Thirsty	185
Waiting	214
Gethsemane	219
Come and Get My Gun	235

ACKNOWLEDGMENTS

The author gratefully acknowledges the following magazines in which the following stories have appeared.

Porter House Review: That's Why God Made Men

Palooka: The Letter My Father Never Wrote Me

805 Lit + Art: This Kind of Man

Streetlight: Come and Get My Gun

Literary Mama: Winning

Panorama, The Journal of Intelligent Travel: Philippi

Dash Journal: Later, That Same Morning

The Chaffin Journal: Life Without Onions

Flash Fiction Magazine: In My Cups

intima, a journal of narrative medicine: Waiting Room

Twisted Vine Lit Arts Journal: Unbroken Things

Tiny Journal: A Brief Catalog of Mostly Forgivable Thoughts

Allium: Gethsemane

in him broods already a taste for mindless violence. All history present in that visage, the child the father of the man.

—Cormac McCarthy, *Blood Meridian*

He lacked the wisdom, and the only way for him to get it was to buy it with Youth; and when wisdom was his, Youth would have been spent in buying it.

—Jack London ("A Piece of Steak")

She didn't understand how men could do those things. What things? he asked, and she said, The things men do. Then he nodded. Oh, he said, those things.

—Tim O'Brien, *The Things They Carried*

Here in this darkness
I know what I've done:
I know all at once who I am.

—Steely Dan, "Don't Take Me Alive"

For Mark Seferian:

oldest friend, ideal reader, unwavering ally

I

THE LETTER MY FATHER NEVER WROTE ME

Listen, son, you have to understand: Everything *was* different, and everything's the same. That's the secret of life. It takes most people their entire lives to learn it. Most people never do. Actually, it isn't the secret of life, it's the secret to dealing with the fact we'll never understand anything. My advice is simple: Don't worry about it. When it's all over, either everything will be explained to us, or nothing happens at all. Either way, we're covered.

  We smoked in movie theaters when I was growing up. You can't do that now. For one thing, no one smokes; for another, no one goes to movies anymore. Can you imagine the sissies of your generation smoking on an airplane? Can you imagine a new mother, today, if somebody lit up next to her? Did you know lawsuits used to be a last resort? Can you imagine eating red meat at least once a day? Can you imagine not counting the number of cocktails you had each week because no one kept count? Can you imagine a world where nobody exercised but no one was fat? Can you imagine a world where you had to marry certain types of women before you could have sex with them? Can you imagine when getting in a fight meant using your fists and not typing words onto a screen? Can you imagine life without insect repellant? Can you imagine a world where there was no such thing as therapy or depression (unless you were rich, and it ran in the family), and if you couldn't handle reality, they put you in an institution? Have you figured out that shame keeps people in line more than any laws ever could? Do you think a car in need of fuel ever complained that gasoline didn't taste good?

Do you understand what I'm saying?

Can you believe we used to eat bologna and processed cheese, and white bread wasn't an adjective, or a political statement? Did you know we didn't know what irony was? Did you know that not being able to change your oil, or fix a flat tire, or repair a leaky faucet meant you couldn't call yourself a man? Can you call yourself a man? Did you know no one used to be gay? But if you wore cologne you were a queer? Can you imagine that armpit sweat and ring around the collar weren't embarrassing, but badges of honor? Do you understand that if skin cancer is the price you pay for not wearing sunscreen, then so be it? Can you imagine a world where people didn't like, let alone trust, color TV? Did you know newspapers used to be delivered in the afternoon? Can you believe professional athletes in the '50s had to get second jobs to make ends meet? Did you realize there was no such thing as endangered species? Can you picture a world where priests were more respected than actors? Do you realize there's never been any accountability, for anything? Do you understand that's why people need to believe in God?

Have you figured out that knowing everything doesn't mean anything?

Did you know wearing a tie to the office was not optional? Or that we used to be able to describe our jobs in one or two

THIS KIND OF MAN

words? (By the way, rich people have always been assholes—get over it.) Could you ever see yourself listening to nine innings on a radio? Listening to a radio at all? Can you imagine a world where you canned food instead of freezing it? Did you know we used to enjoy when movies had happy endings? Did you know that dogs, just like the people who owned them, used to die because there was no money or options to prolong their lives? Can you believe people used to turn their underwear inside out to use them a second time? Do you think all those fuckers on Wall Street got spanked as kids, or did they get put in "time out"? Did you know the underclass used to go to college for free because it was called the military? Did you know I learned more from kicking someone's ass than I ever learned in school? Did you know I learned more from getting my ass kicked than anything else? Have you ever had your ass kicked? (We know you've never kicked anyone's ass.)

Do you understand what a toll it takes loving things you don't believe or even want?

Do you understand if fathers talked about everything the way everyone always wants them to, wives, and children, and friends might like them more, but would never respect them? Are you aware this is the sacrifice required when you become a father? Do you know that we figured out how to be fathers, and husbands, and employees after we already had skin in the game? Do you understand this is why we despise your generation? Do you realize it's why we pity you, too?

Can we agree, finally, that if I've done my job as a man, as a father, I won't have to tell you any of these things?

THIS KIND OF MAN

The ground beef has been mixed with two eggs, salted, and shaped. My hands thoroughly scrubbed with soap and water, I'm ready for action. Next step is going to the grocery store for the rest of the ingredients.

What kind of man does this?

A man with a lot of time to kill.

My wife was like most women. She would ensure she had everything she needed before preparing a meal. But even before our second child was born, she'd already cooked enough dinners to lose all fondness for the routine. Food became another chore—fuel which fed a family; another task to accomplish with as little effort as possible. The more time it required meant less time to do anything else, and something else always needed to be done. The bathrooms wouldn't clean themselves; the dishes wouldn't put themselves away; the carpets wouldn't miraculously get vacuumed.

If I didn't comprehend all this then, I do now.

I could and, according to my daughter, should, just hire a cleaning service. It's only me, though, and the house remains pretty manageable, at least compared to the days when four of us were living in it. I tell her I can handle things; that this isn't about the money. And it isn't. The truth is, I have too much of what my wife always wanted more of: time.

My wife considered it an unforgivable lapse of discipline if she had to make separate trips to the store in a single week. Her shopping lists were legendary, almost scientific equations, precise and unerring. Years of trial and error led to an exact awareness of how much milk, bread, toilet paper, and detergent our family used. We seldom had extra supplies but never seemed to run out of anything. I can't recall ever needing a razor, or a Q-tip, or a tissue. There's a sort of method there anyone might emulate. Not especially organized when we first got married, my wife became an expert at efficiency. Housewives from our generation learned how to balance budgets and resources in ways that should embarrass the clowns in today's government.

When my wife got sick, I learned how to cook. I hated it. Prepared food or frozen meals were fine with me. Maybe I was busy doing other things (by that point I was doing everything), or simply took no pleasure in eating. It's difficult to enjoy familiar flavors when you live with someone who can hardly recall what they taste like. When they've reached the point where all the machinery keeping them alive has turned them into a machine. My wife once told me she envied my morning bowel movements, something I never imagined hearing one person say to another.

I was a terrible cook, like most men from my generation. It should have been easier, following a formula for consistent results. Nevertheless, it took longer than I'd like to acknowledge, becoming comfortable in my own kitchen. Then again, I couldn't have become an accountant the same day I learned to add and subtract. Anything done with some degree of competence involves practice, and a great deal of failure.

I'm not sure if I enjoy cooking now so much as I appreciate overseeing a process from start to finish. My son makes a good living, but he'd save a lot more if he didn't eat out or order-in for every meal. In fairness, I would have done the same if I'd never settled down.

I'd explain this to him if we still spoke, but he'll figure it out, eventually.

Or maybe he won't have to. We shouldn't wish for our children to be exactly like us, especially when it entails making the same mistakes.

What kind of man doesn't speak to his son?

A man whose son won't speak to him.

I used to spend weeks with difficult clients, doing everything possible to convince them and still occasionally lose the account. When I cook, I know exactly what I need, the precise time, materials, and effort expected. If we were able to know what was expected of us, what we should expect, I reckon most people would be perfectly content.

My wife and I always joked about how I would die first. Which of my friends, I'd ask, will be the one who flirts with you? Which ones would you consider going on a date with? Would you ever remarry? What on earth would you do with all the extra time? I never admitted it, but it was that last question that caused me the most distress. That was the one I wasn't sure I wanted the answer to.

What kind of man worries his wife will be at peace when he's gone?

THIS KIND OF MAN

Any man who is honest, I say.

Women from my generation are capable of losing sleep over one simple question: How will my husband manage, living alone? Men worry that, after so much time spent serving and fretting over us, our wives would relish an autonomy they're unaccustomed to. Perhaps even regret the wasted years, the missed opportunities, etc.

Thank God for religion. Without its mechanisms of control, our hospitals would become retirement homes for chronic alcoholics. Our streets would be overrun with once highly functioning husbands who can't do anything other than work, sleep, eat, and sometimes screw. It's safe to say, if not for religion—and the self-regulating shame it imparts—my own mother would have been there too, once I was out of the picture. Religion, money, and viable options: Without the first and with either of the following two, how many wives would stick it out?

I know there must have been times my wife saw greener grass on the other side of our marriage, and I can't blame her too much. However, if she had followed through, she wouldn't have had a partner by her side when for better turned to worse.

Or maybe she would have. Maybe she would never have gotten cancer at all. We always figured I'd be the first to go.

Losing your wife tends to complicate your feelings about the afterlife. If it's there, she's there, and someday, God willing, I'll be there, too.

But so will everyone else. That means God—not to mention countless strangers—will know everything. They'll have seen all the fights, the times I wouldn't speak to her, all the lies (mostly small ones), that one time at the Christmas party that I was too drunk to remember exactly what happened anyway, etc. Her parents will have seen the way their grandson and son-in-law squared off in the garage, just after their daughter's funeral; the day my son finally felt he had the right to pop off about how miserable I made his mother, as if he was the one wiping stains off the bathroom floor, or double-washing sheets soaked with sweat and puke, or keeping track of the meds, or driving to another appointment, or sitting alone in the waiting room bracing for bad news— it's always bad news no matter what you think you're prepared to hear.

What kind of man would trade places with his dying wife?

Well, it's complicated.

No sane person would want to suffer like that. It's difficult enough dealing with disease from a mostly safe distance. Still, once it became obvious how our story was going to end, I won't say I didn't envy her a little.

We don't get to see our own funerals. We never know what everyone will say, what they really think of us. And unless there's some type of eternity, we never will. Unless we die first, unless we have the type of death that attracts a crowd. You expect sympathy, but it's the ones who show up that tell you everything you need to know. I couldn't believe the people who came to say goodbye, not just the viewings, but those last few days. People we hadn't seen in years, people I had frankly forgotten about, people I know would never have come to see me.

Who will come to see me? I can count on my daughter, even though she lives in a separate time zone. I don't think my son will even be there to see me buried, but he'll have to live with that, just like I did, not attending my father's funeral. I'm pretty much at peace with it.

Of course, I was relieved so many people showed up for my wife. I know it meant a great deal to her. It provided proof she was loved, that her life *mattered*. Most of us won't get that same opportunity. And if we do, we might not like what we discover.

Even when her bones hurt, she worried about me. My bones hurt when I breathe, she said. And she still told me she worried about me. Mostly, she reminded me everything would be okay, that I deserved a break after this ordeal, that I'd enjoy my space, that we'd never have to fight over the remote control anymore, that kind of crap. But she really did worry. Her concern was the one thing, besides her pain, that I remember most clearly about those last weeks.

Although I saw her give birth, and breastfeed, and get up in the night with sick kids, and make bag lunches, and wash dirty underwear, and maintain every important relationship, and send out birthday cards to relatives, and put everyone she loved before herself, even as she lay dying, it wasn't until then that I finally understood the real difference between husbands and wives, fathers and mothers, men and women.

What kind of man doesn't have some regrets?

A man who has tried his best, whatever that means.

A man who owns what he's done, whatever that is. I know I was there when it mattered most, and my wife said it meant everything. But did that make up for all the other things? The wasted opportunities, the forgotten slights, the countless times

I could have told her something sweet, the times I made her cry, the days and nights I wasn't there?

The only promise I ever cared about keeping was the one I made to myself when I swore I wouldn't be like my old man.

I saw him do things, and say things, and mostly *not* say things, but I don't think he ever entertained a moment of doubt. He checked all the boxes men of his time were supposed to: When he wasn't working, he was sleeping, or in church, or building something, or repairing something else. He was the only man I've known who didn't appear to have an imagination. I don't think he ever envisioned anything other than what he expected to happen. I couldn't forgive him for this, and now I'd give anything to experience what that feels like. Especially if there's no afterlife. If it all ends, what's the point of all this wasted thought? All this useless energy convincing ourselves that anything matters…

What kind of man will the neighbors, or paramedics, or whoever find, when someone finally finds him—as though he simply fell asleep on the same couch he'd slept on during so many forgettable TV shows, in the same suit he hadn't worn since his wife's funeral, an emptied bottle of pills he'd stolen from the hospice nurse and hidden away, without a note, or phone call, or farewell, a half-made meatloaf on the counter, some kind of signal or surrender?

A man who hopes he's not around to ask or have to answer any further questions.

WINNING

I am not my father's son.

This is what my old man would tell me, throughout my childhood, when I disappointed him. In hindsight, and in fairness to us both, it wasn't that often, but when I was growing up it seemed like he was saying this, or some variation of it, constantly.

"I don't even know where you came from," he'd sigh, holding another report card like it was a dead rodent. I had no trouble with English and History—the sissy subjects—but was hopeless at Math and Science—the real subjects. This was a personal affront to his sensibilities.

"I should sue the hospital for malpractice," he'd say, shaking his head. "They gave me the *dumb* one by mistake."

"There is no way you're mine," he'd insist, especially when it came to anything sports related. Tough love was the only love. I was a half-decent soccer player and could usually hit my weight in baseball, but who can't in grade school?

My mother was also culpable, only able to provide him one child, defying his designs as well as his Catholic aspirations. Given one or two more opportunities, the better-looking, left-brained reincarnation of the varsity wrestler he'd once been would have at least been conceivable.

When they got divorced, he won custody. This was exceedingly rare in those days. I imagine it was a fairly acrimonious trial because after it they never spoke, as far as I know. It's not like she disappeared so much as she did a do-over: remarried within a year and relocated to the other side of the country.

It was easy to blame him for her absence, and I often did, once I came to understand other kids had something I didn't. Eventually I realized, he, too, was deprived; he never remarried, and on a couple of occasions he mentioned that he still loved my mother. She left him with a son and that was it, just the two of us, no mediators or distractions. We both seemed to assume, if not accept, we'd spend the rest of our lives figuring one another out.

***

My father needed to compete.

That may sound extreme, or trite, but the vitality he conjured from competing was a force that kept him alive. In a sense, his life was an extended competition: He watched his old man battle the absence of employment as their family stared down poverty. Later, he was the first of five siblings to attend college, made possible through scholarships and loans. If these early obstacles forged the resilience that made him a successful businessman, they also provided the perennial chip, slung over both shoulders, which pitted him against the world.

He had a heart murmur—which I was not aware of until later in my own life. It was detected in childhood, so the specter of premature death colored his outlook before it had any

THIS KIND OF MAN

business being there. It became a condition he kept at bay by simply *beating* it; ignoring it, each day a victory that prevented it from beating him. Moreover, he mocked the condition by the lifestyle he chose: He made himself tough.

This carried over into all aspects of his existence, at work or at play. I grew up watching the Red Sox with him, a pathology that only augmented the household tension; each game would dictate his mood. This is not to say he'd necessarily be in *good* spirits if they won, but if they lost? It was best not to be in his vicinity. He had to vent, to take his frustration out on something, and I was made a target by simply being there. As always, sports and being in control were the things that drove him to distraction, and the only things that could restore him. It was not unusual for neighbors to see him out in our driveway after 10 p.m. shooting baskets, his own brand of therapy.

***

As far back as I can remember, my father and I were competing.

I was branded with competitiveness like a steer, and whenever I'd compete, that ugly scar became visible. No one likes a poor sport, and God knows I was as poor of a sport as they come. Of course, the only thing worse than losing was dealing with my old man when I lost. So, in a sense I was always competing with him.

Paternal neglect was never an issue for me. My pops was at every game, every practice. He even watched from inside the house, pacing and chain-smoking, when I kicked the ball in the yard.

He was there when I scored my first soccer goal. I was seven years old, and after the game he took me to 7-Eleven and bought me a large Slurpee, announcing to everyone in the store that *his* son was a winner.

The next week my team lost the game two-to-one; I didn't score our goal. In fact, I blew my chance at being a hero by kicking a last-minute penalty shot right into the goalkeeper's arms. My father didn't say a word as I walked off the field, and he wouldn't look at me as we drove home. I stared out the window, shaking with my effort to hold back tears. I never cried in front of him, it only made everything worse. He seemed to sense my distress and pulled up to 7-Eleven.

"Wait in the car," he said.

He returned with a large Slurpee in his hand and set it down on the dashboard in front of me. When I happily reached out, he grabbed it and looked at me like I'd just broken a window.

"What do you think you're doing?"

I looked at him in confusion.

"You'll get a Slurpee when you deserve one," he said, placing the cup back on the dashboard. "Just stare at it and think about why you lost."

Even though I successfully held back the tears until we got home, he still won, as always. I practiced penalty kicks for the rest of the afternoon.

***

I became a good athlete as I grew older.

THIS KIND OF MAN

Before I was ten, I already played on travel soccer and basketball teams. I swam every day in the summer, and every winter morning my old man would awaken me at 5 a.m. to swim laps before school.

Anytime I had a chance to succeed was an opportunity to see my father happy, so I was at once driven and selfish. I was not particularly well-liked by my teammates, but winning was more important than camaraderie.

One memory—the only constant aside from his presence at every athletic event—is the annual bike ride we'd take each summer vacation. We always spent the last week of August at Martha's Vineyard, which was at that time still a best-kept secret of sorts. The highlight of each trip was when we rented bicycles and ferried over to Chappaquiddick, the neighboring island. To this day it's still mostly known as the place Ted Kennedy ruined his chance to be president.

Those bike rides were typically a respite, a peaceful farewell to summer. They were the calm highlights of each vacation, until the year I turned thirteen and initiated a new tradition.

We were about a mile from the ferry and, out of nowhere, I challenged him to a race. Without a sound he was five yards ahead of me, peddling like a lunatic. He beat me by about ten seconds and near the end, when I realized I had no chance to win, I began coasting, pretending to have lost interest. He taunted me the entire ferry ride back.

"Maybe next year, boy," he said. Each time he laughed I fantasized throwing him overboard.

He beat me the next year, and he beat me badly. I never could figure it out. I was convinced I could bike circles around him, just like I knew I was a better basketball player. But for some reason, whenever I was out there with him, I moved in slow motion.

As we each grew older, I came to understand my father had his own reasons for wanting to win. By beating me he could maintain the ideal father-son equilibrium: I was still young enough to remain in his shadow, and he was still young enough to keep me there. No son truly grows up until he grows out of his old man's shadow.

It wasn't until I turned seventeen that I finally beat him.

It was an overcast day, and we said practically nothing to each other as we rode around. Over the years, even the novelty of our pre-race ride dissipated. I scarcely admired the scenery as I once did; now I concentrated on pacing myself, focusing on the road directly in front of me. I noticed the pebbles and beach's sand that the rain had scattered along the road. It had drizzled all morning, but the precipitation ceased just as we left our cottage. I took it as a harbinger of victory, confident this was finally my year.

Right from the start I knew I was going to win. I felt locked in like never before as the teenage adrenaline surged through my body. Before the race was halfway over, I could hear my father grunting with exertion. This pleased me immensely; I knew there was no way he could maintain the pace I was setting. Not this time.

It was beautiful to look back and see him twenty yards behind me as I approached the old whaling house that always served as our finish line. I wanted to make the moment as memorable as possible, so I threw my arms in the air and tossed my head back like I was clinching the Tour de France.

I crossed the invisible line, eyes closed, mouth open in a cry of triumph, not noticing the patch of wet sand in the middle of the road. I felt myself rushing forward while my leg became tangled up in the chain. I tore most of the skin off my left arm as I was dragged several feet down the road. I sprained my ankle when the bike landed on top of me, but I was lucky not to hit my head—we never wore helmets in those days.

The pain was significant, but I could handle that. The worst part was having to stand up on my own and support myself on the broken bike; my father had ridden right past me.

***

Things were never the same between us after that.

I had proven I could beat him, and he had made it clear that he resented me for it. The familiar tension was replaced by something previously unimaginable: indifference.

My father had carried me through math for three years, helping me with all my courses. At the beginning of my senior year, he laid down the new law. "You need to figure this out. The world will swallow you whole if you keep depending on other people."

Naturally, I needed to prove I could succeed without him; I paid a tutor to get me through trigonometry.

When basketball season started, he no longer attended every game. I was relieved at first, then pretended I didn't care, but it seemed unnatural not to watch him watching me. To spite him, I applied only to West Coast colleges, convinced that once I was gone, he'd regret it.

I likely would have drifted completely apart from him, but as usually happens with families, a crisis brought us together. About two weeks into the New Year, when snowfall was no longer a novelty, my father had a heart attack.

I heard him out in the driveway, shooting free throws. I offered him a game of H.O.R.S.E. but eventually, inevitably, it turned into a one-on-one game. It was frigid outside, the type of day where your hands become numb if you stop moving them. By the last game the ball felt like a frozen tire, but we always finished what we started.

All his advantages had steadily been neutralized over the years: I was now a few inches taller, and he wasn't in the same shape he'd been before turning fifty. I drove past him for a backward lay-up, laughing the way he'd once laughed at me when he was bigger and taller. I felt like a bird that lived long enough to mock the older, declawed cat that had once tormented it.

"Game point," I said.

He didn't respond; he glared at me and motioned for the ball. I bounced it to him and he took it on the run, trying to duplicate the move I'd just made. He jumped too early and the ball flew out of his hand, rolling into the bushes. I began running my mouth as he went to retrieve it, and he abruptly dropped to one knee.

"Oh," he gasped.

THIS KIND OF MAN

I figured he'd twisted his ankle. Then he collapsed onto the driveway, holding his side. I ran over and noticed his face soaked with sweat and his eyes squeezed shut.

"Pop, what is it?"

"Call…"

"Pop!"

"Ambulance…"

I sprinted into the house and made the call. I remember desperately wishing my mother was there.

When I came back outside, the look on his face was somewhere between anger and embarrassment. The only thing worse than lying supine, looking up helplessly at his son, was the idea of dying. I knelt down and put my hand under his damp head. He seemed to grin, as if in relief or gratitude. I realized it was pain.

I heard the ambulance approaching in the distance.

My father was trying to say something. He reached up and grabbed weakly at my shirt sleeve. I leaned down and put my ear to his mouth. As the ambulance roared into our driveway his voice was barely audible, a whisper. But I heard him.

"Not yet," he said. "Not yet…"

***

As he predicted in the driveway, my old man had plenty of fight left. In fact, he was in the hospital less than a week. "This is no place to recover," he said. The nurses thought he was kidding around, but I knew better. Of course, the risk of another attack was significant, so the doctor's verdict was simple and stark: No more cigarettes and no more sports. It was like a death sentence disguised as an admonition; I felt genuinely sorry for him.

For the next few months, he brooded and sulked around the house, like a tiger confined to a cage. He kicked his nicotine habit (another competition he needed to win), but immediately packed on some unwanted pounds. To keep in shape, he rescued the stationary bicycle that had been collecting dust in our basement for more than a decade. When the weather got warmer, he would go on solitary bike rides, and before long he looked as healthy as ever.

He started coming to my games again once soccer season began, and it seemed right to see him back in the stands, where he belonged.

It was a great spring for me. Our team won the district championship and the day after Easter I got my acceptance letter to play college soccer on a full ride. I called my old man and he sounded typically unimpressed, but he came home from work with a bottle of champagne and a six pack of imported beer. After dinner we got drunk, him telling me we could finally celebrate like men. He kept staring at me, and each time I'd look back at him he'd pick up the letter and repeat the same thing, like a mantra. "This is the realization of all our dreams."

I was at once unburdened and amazed: For that one night it was almost like we were friends.

As the summer wound down, I looked forward to our vacation with a mixture of excitement and uncertainty, knowing this was my final week with him before leaving home for the first time.

***

THIS KIND OF MAN

The last thing on my mind that day was racing.

We took our time, slowly navigating the silent shoreline. I was absorbed in my own thoughts as he cruised ahead of me, whistling to himself. It occurred to me that I was unprepared to be without my old man, something I would never have imagined a year before.

At some point I passed him, he immediately overtook me, no longer whistling.

Instinctively I pumped my legs and regained the advantage.

I glanced sideways, but he wasn't looking at me. His eyes were set straight ahead as he pushed forward—in front—and began peddling in earnest.

Ever since his heart attack we hadn't physically challenged one another. I figured we had outgrown it. But as the breeze whipped around our faces, I realized we would never outgrow it and we could never be friends. We were too much alike.

I lowered my head and began setting a pace, breathing through my nose. Just like every race in the past there were no words, no acknowledgment of the other one's presence.

His new routines had paid off: He was cruising along and I had to push myself to keep up with him. From behind, I could see him straining; I noticed the sweat soaking his shirt and the improved tone of his calves. I took a deep breath and readied myself for a final push. As I pulled even with him, I thought I could hear him muttering under his breath. Was he motivating himself? Cursing me? Praying? Whatever he was—or wasn't—saying, I understood in that moment that he needed to win. It wasn't because he could no longer beat me that he looked so desperate; it was because he *could* win that he was peddling as though this was the last time he'd ever mount a bike.

But I found myself pushing harder because a voice still choking from the weight of memory reminded me of all the times he should have let me win.

I looked over at my father, then beyond him at the water. Nothing had changed: The waves still rolled in and we were still moving down the road, rushing to stay in the same place.

As we approached the whaling house, I made a noise I'd never heard before. It was, at once, an exhalation of air, history, and a familiar expectation. At that same moment, I gently squeezed my handbrake—just enough to slow myself down. I coasted past the finish line directly behind my father.

We dismounted our bikes and stood there, looking at everything but each other. I waited for him to say something, to ask the question I knew he had to ask. Finally, he did.

"Did you try to win?"

I never could lie to my old man, so there was no way I could look him in the eye. I didn't say a word and cycled past him without looking back. As much as I wanted to, I didn't turn around. I didn't need to. If I had, I know I would have seen something I'd always hoped to see more of during my childhood: his smile.

***

The day I left for college I watched my old man cry for the first and last time. As I got on the plane, I felt guilty because I knew I was leaving him behind, and alone.

THIS KIND OF MAN

About a week before midterms, just as I was getting accustomed to my new life at school, my father died. It was his heart again.

***

I am not my son's father.

When I found out I couldn't have a child of my own, I first thought it was fate. Then I understood that it was yet another challenge: a different one, a good one. After being told so often I was adopted, it was like my pops was preparing me, in his ironic way, to be a foster parent. I grin constantly, imagining how my old man would find more ways not to recognize himself in me, a father.

I hear my friends lament what a bunch of babies we are raising these days. No spanking, no stern words, trophies for everyone, no preparation for the remorseless reality awaiting them in the real world, etc.

Maybe they're right. But I've noticed no one hands out awards to adults, and life is a succession of battles not measured on scoreboards. If winning is the only thing that matters, then most of us are losing, every single day. And I don't know if I'll be around when my boy is old enough to be on his own. Until he is, I want him to see me on the sidelines, content no matter what the score is. I want him to hear me say so many of the things I longed to hear when I was his age. I need him to be unafraid of failure and know he will never let his old man down.

NOW'S THE TIME

If not now, when?

He knows the answer. It's all in his head: every reason, every word, every retort, all the things he might have said, or should have said. Or never had the right words to say. He always would find them, after (in his head), when it was too late. That's the story of his life, he thinks. Every time the wrong decision, or even worse, the inability to make one.

He's still not certain now's the time to do what he's doing. Walking, outside, in this weather? He'd already passed the familiar fire warning sign: A big Smokey the Bear, holding his shovel and announcing that the danger today was VERY HIGH. Usually, if not always, it was low, or occasionally moderate; a straightforward, stark HIGH would be considered a big deal. *Very High?* Unprecedented, and he hasn't missed a summer here in more than two decades. Maybe they were making a point, a little scare tactic going a long way for irresponsible smokers or potential arsonists who might let off a firecracker at the wrong time in the wrong place. No one could deny it was hot: above ninety in a town that still treated air conditioning as a luxury. Hell, most houses hadn't gotten cable TV until the turn of the century. Of course, all the new houses

THIS KIND OF MAN

had AC and every other modern luxury—but these were a new class of people, the ones transforming this once obscure destination into the worst kind of poser's paradise.

If not today, when?

Need to get those steps in, he thinks sardonically, looking down at how tight his t-shirt is, keeping his beer gut strapped in like a hyperactive toddler in a car seat. Beer gut? It was also a pizza, chips, fast food, and not enough fruit & veggies, healthy living is for faggots gut (Oops, can't say *that* word anymore, of course. Even though he'd said it all his life, had been called it so often it was like taking a piss or brushing his teeth—just part of another boring and predictable day. He wasn't even bullied, back in the day, because none of the bigger and brighter boys suspected he was anything less than straight. They regarded him, correctly, as another pockmarked loser lusting after girls who'd be offended if you asked them out; girls who'd be nauseated if they thought you ever jerked off thinking about them. He didn't wear the word so much as a badge of honor as proof he was safely anonymous: not the antelope in the front or rear of the herd, not the first one the tigers would target when it was dinner time.)

Don't do the crime if you can't do the time.

How many times had he heard his father say this? Before he split, that is. Who knew what his old man was looking like these days. Was he still jogging—putting in that roadwork, as he used to call it—or had he let the law of gravity eventually do to him what it does to just about everyone?

It occurs to him that he hadn't cared about what his old man was doing or where he was, much less how he looked, for a long while. He could almost kid himself into thinking he wasn't still nurturing all sorts of hostility about how his father had left him and his mother. How he'd cashed in for newer models with less issues, upshifting to the second act of his life. Maybe he'd gone in an entirely different direction; maybe he was a priest or about to run for president. Mostly, he thinks: fuck him, wherever and whatever he was.

Cars keep passing him at a steady clip in both directions: all headed someplace or back to where they left. So many cars, so many individual lives, all with stories. His old man had a story. *He* had a story. It's his awareness of this fact that has caused him unreasonable agitation, especially lately. The idea that he can (should, or shouldn't) take charge of his own narrative—the things he can change —or else accept having no power of influence. To acknowledge all these potential scenarios is, in theory, possible, but if you don't have faith in a higher power or your own ability to do anything that matters, it leaves you in a sort of desperate paralysis. You're nowhere, nothing. And then what do you do?

Count the cars.

THIS KIND OF MAN

He counts the cars that pass him. Every other one is an SUV or something north of $50K per model. These machines less a means of transportation than passports; tokens of the same lifestyles that made white fences (repainted each season) and grass even cows couldn't eat routine, obligatory. Fake toys for fake people leading fake existences, all made possible by a fake system that rewarded fakeness. The kind of world no one ever asked his permission to become a part of.

Almost time until the sun explodes.

It's hotter than he'd ever remembered it being. If you listened to the lunatics on the news, the earth was suddenly unlivable and man had caused all this heat and drought, accelerating some apocalypse or implosion. Was it in fact hotter than it had been when he was a kid, or even a few years ago? It seemed like it, but how many things seemed different than when he was younger? Maybe kids don't notice these things because if they get hot, they jump in a pool, or a lake, or the splash of a fire hydrant, whatever. You get sunburned, and bitten by mosquitoes, and don't get to eat all the ice cream you want, or your favorite team never wins, but none of it matters because it's all play and no worries. Maybe, he thinks, that's the true reason retards seem so happy: eternally in the child's mind, no bills or dates or jobs or friends or global warming to worry about. (Can't say that word either, but it was another in a long list of insults he'd grown accustomed to hearing, once upon a time.)

A horn blast disrupts his reflections, and he looks up, already too late to tell if it's someone honking at him, or at another driver, or just some asshole letting the world know he's there (he's certain, it's definitely a *he*).

It was something his father would do—an alpha male move, since men can't trumpet like elephants or roar like lions. A way of making sure everyone (anyone) is aware: *I'm here.* To do something like this would require either a confidence or obliviousness he can't fathom. To genuinely not care what anyone else thinks? Even wealthy people don't have that privilege. Especially wealthy people. He knew from wealthy people, having lived as a decidedly non-wealthy person in this town —a place that had become more popular, more expensive, less hospitable to those without means (*stupid money*, his father used to say) at a seemingly ridiculous pace. It did, he figures, mirror what was happening in the rest of the country (the rest of the world?)—not just the haves taking more and pissing on the heads of the have-nots, but a general acknowledgment that *this was the way it was*, and always had been; America was finally catching up with what happens, inevitably, with all empires. The only people working hard, day after day, were the underemployed trying to stay afloat, and the one-percenters making sure they kept a stranglehold on everything they could (and couldn't yet) afford. The worst part, he figured, was that it wasn't even personal; *this* was the world people voted for and fought wars to preserve.

"On your left!"

THIS KIND OF MAN

He half-freezes and watches the two women pass him, obvious tourists on rented bikes, taking in the sights and working up a sweat. So they could cool off in their private pools before firing up the blender for margaritas; maybe before they showered and got dressed up for a night on the town, or else some catered affair, all a business expense or tax write-off. The restaurant he used to work for made most of their profits with this kind of clientele, people who had the means to outsource everything, including the preparation and clean-up; their only job to eat, drink, and be perfect. Or miserable. Either way, strictly business. His mother had told him that was the gig to pursue—being the one shuttling the food or packing it up after, the kind of job that didn't oblige heavy lifting (literally or figuratively) and often came with huge cash tips under the table (strictly business). But there was one reason—aside from the fact he didn't want, under any circumstances, to be around these people—that he understood he'd never be seriously considered for that job: he was, once again, trapped in the middle, a native speaker who had neither the education nor the looks to put this class of people at peace, and not poor enough (i.e., white) to be fully exploited. The foreign workers, here seasonally because living year-round was financially out of the question, arguably had it best. They came in hot and left before it got cold (figuratively but especially literally). Not necessarily the ones exploited by the hotels—that was shit work to be sure, but all those lucky or attractive enough to gain employment in the hospitality industry, being in the presence of this plastic fantasy.

If you can't beat them…

He thinks about the girl at the store, the one that *could* have been, but probably not. The one he had gotten to know in that unique way where you see someone often enough to "know" them, but without knowing the first thing about them. How many times a week did he see her and exchange pleasantries as he checked out, his beer or snacks tiding him over for a day or two? She was younger, part of the new wave of worker (Lithuanian? Portuguese?). That one time, having rung him up and nodded goodbye too many times to count, she eyeballed his 12 pack and said: "nice choice." Suddenly there were countless ways for him to play this. "Too bad I have to drink them alone," he might have said. No, too forceful, also kind of admitting he didn't have anyone (female or male) to hang out with. "I'll save a few for you," he might have tried, but would she have understood the humor, could he have managed to quickly follow up his comment with an invite? "What's your brand?" he should have attempted; anyone could pull *that* off. Easy, a lay-up. He could have gone harder with "What kind does your boyfriend like?", something that bold requiring a definitive response, unfolding a whole history of possibilities. Instead, he'd weakly nodded his head and held out his hand for change.

And after that he had to replay how he'd blown it every time he checked out, because he always had less than eight items, and she was always working the quick check-out aisle, too new or dumb to have been promoted to the regular lanes, waiting on grumpy housewives or Ivy League nannies or semi-aliens, like her, who were combining odd jobs and under the

THIS KIND OF MAN

counter wages, inevitably for wealthy, wasp-y bitches, the kind of people who played croquet in their manicured fortresses.

Time to water the grass.

There were exactly two types of lawns on this island: withered crab grass forever in need of more rain—or man-made hydration—than were on offer or affordable, and the expansive lawns so green they looked like carpets—more science experiment than actual color. The types of lawns adjoining with properties that belonged to the people for whom no expense was an obstacle. The kind of people who made (or, more likely, inherited) the kind of money that made these fabricated lifestyles their own kind of scientific experiment.

He watches the two girls approach: late teens, cheerleaders or class clowns biding time before college, or marriage, or whatever fill-in-the-blank fairy tale their parents had already paid for. They could have been daughters of the girls who'd alternately tormented and ignored him when he was their age.

"Excuse me," he says.

"Yeah?"

"What time is it?"

They look at him, then at each other.

"You've got a watch on," one of them says.

"That's my whole point," he replies, grinning.

They give him a look he's familiar with: confusion tinged with, well, no other word for it: disgust. They walk on and he pauses, adjusts his backpack, then keeps going in the opposite direction, very much still the main character in the story he's writing about himself.

No time to whine.

Speaking of which, maybe it did taste good, the stuff he used to bring by the tub-load to the recycling bin the summer he bussed tables at the country club. Fancy pants. Five-hundred-dollar dinners for a family of four, featuring a round or two of cocktails, apps all around—usually shrimp cocktail or clam chowder—salads, entrees, a bottle or three of wine, desserts for the kids, after-dinner drinks, usually something undrinkable (he knew from sampling too many floaters—the swill warming like sewage in a snifter). Bottles of vino, even the cheapest shit at least $50 a pop, usually upward of one-to-two hundred. And the big timers, five car families with friends and no worries in the world, ordering like they had to spend their money before it burned holes in their bank accounts. I'll huff, and I'll puff, and I'll burn your house down, he thinks, recalling all those faceless monsters, the unquenchable hatred he felt for them, and his co-workers, especially the wait staff, the girls in particular, all slumming it for the summer before heading back to school and taking classes to learn how to take over the world. God how he despised them, unable to fathom how they lived enough to envy them.

THIS KIND OF MAN

Time for a wild card?

He thinks about hitch-hiking—speaking of old-fashioned ideas. He remembers his father saying: This whole island used to be a haven for hitchhikers. To and from the beach, to the grocery store, the package store, you name it. It was a much different world then. A whiter world (facts are facts no matter how out of fashion). That was one thing he *had* figured out: Yes, back in the bad old days that seemed so good now it was whites who worked the unthinkable jobs, being condescended to without shame or exception. But there was a type of understanding; there was still the conceivable possibility, however illusory, that someday, you too could join the ranks of these elite stiffs. That's what he realized made him kindred spirits with the displaced ditch diggers and fresh out of luck farmers: There were now people not only willing to do that work, but do it cheaper and with enthusiasm. How can we expect to ever change *that* pattern? Not happening. The world keeps turning and finds new ways to make things suck more for people like him. He sticks up his thumb and makes a bet with himself: if anyone picks me up, I'll tell him (obviously it will be a *him*) to take me to the water. Maybe I'll even jump in, fully clothed. It'll be a plot twist, a revision to the work in progress.

Time to get real.

"There's college," his mother had said. Often.

"Out of the question," he'd responded a few times; he never said—or felt the need to say—anything further. Too expensive. Too different. Too much of it, too little of me. Every excuse in the book, especially the good ones.

"Heck, there's junior college. We called it JUCO when I was your age," she laughed. He never laughed back, not one time.

Time to lose your mind.

Sure, he'd gone down the rabbit hole. How could he not? It was all right there, just waiting for anyone to find it. Online, all those too-easy explanations for why everything seemed forever out of reach. Especially the stuff served up like a free buffet for people like, well, like him. Angry, alienated, alone. He looked for—and at first, found—something like solidarity. Not understanding or even companionship (these people were not easy on the eyes, and that was just the dudes), but a *feeling*, proof he wasn't alone. That other people also saw this lame joke for what it was, that they understood the fix was in and the fuckheads in places of power spent all their time making sure it stayed that way, and every day it became less reasonable to assume (much less hope) anything would ever change. Unless, you know, *revolution*, but that's the kind of game where your own life is collateral damage, and, he knew (and came to see, in the lower depths of his rabbit hole) that not many of these weekend warriors, these wannabe insurrectionists, were going to pony up if and when shit got real. These chumps, he knew, were very willing and able to fuck around, but very few of them wanted to find out.

THIS KIND OF MAN

Time to tell the truth.

"Let me tell you the secret," he imagines his old man saying, checking in maybe from the west coast, or somewhere across the sea, or right here in this town ruled by people from different zip codes. "You want to know what's out there? You've got to cut the cord and jump in."

Yeah, if you say so, he fancies replying, smirk frozen on his face. "I'm serious," the man who'd ceased to be his father would insist. "You have to be willing to do anything and leave anything—even your family." Like you did, he'd say, and his old man would look at him as though he had the solution to every secret ever conceived, but simply wasn't sure he could trust the young man not following in his footsteps to grasp. "Here's the good news or bad news, depending on what you're made of," his father would say, a parting shot masquerading as parental concern. "The better life is a members-only club, and only one person can keep you out if it. If you're willing to do whatever it takes, you might surprise them all. You might even surprise yourself." No, that's another thing he had come to a certain, painful peace with: There were no surprises in this life.

Time to talk to God.

What about it, God, what do you have to say for yourself, he doesn't say and had never said, because as stupid as he knows he is, he isn't helpless enough to hope there's a friendly old ghost handing out cards, like a dealer for the fanciest spot on the strip. He's seen enough during his short life to remain mostly content staying in his corner, playing the nickel slots, knowing it is all rigged. What else was he supposed to do, punch the sky or jump off a bridge?

Time's up.

He's arrived, finally, at the store. All the beer in the world's waiting for him, perfectly chilled, all the bottles of wine he'd never had sufficient curiosity, or nerve, to sample. The protein on display, priced by the pound: bleached chicken breasts and steaks sprayed red to attain that fake freshness. Every kind of junk food imaginable: baked or light or full-on fat boy, with dips and salsas, everything packaged and canned and sponsored by some type of movie or mascot, all of it an assembly line that lets you measure how you are living. All arranged to keep you from thinking about dying.

Time to tell everyone what time it is.

He walks in, his work boots wet (with sweat? Blood?), reminding him how far he's come to get here. It's the mid-to-late afternoon lull, customers who'd gotten a late start on their day and were running behind, against the clock, or the ones ahead of the game, getting their chores done, taking care of business so they could relax and enjoy the spoils of all the hard, meaningless work they'd been doing all their lives. And right there, on Register One, is his girl. Not enough seniority to work one of the slower registers; seemingly trapped for life—or at least this summer—at Eight Items or Less, which meant serving the simpletons with half-full carts thinking they were putting one over on the system, knowing they'd never be called out. Getting back at the Man or whatever it was that motivated them to cheat or assume their time was more important than anyone else's.

"Now's the time," he says, mostly to himself.

She looks up and gives him her usual greeting: the slight nod, a kind of half gesture—less or more than business cordial, depending on the day. Today it's tough to tell: her eyes don't linger for that extra half-second that signified a good day, that signified she was in a good mood. On a day that was definitively bad, there would be the briefest of looks, an embarrassment to call it actual eye contact. Today though, it's impossible to discern, so he takes it for exactly what it is: the look someone on the clock gives someone else when their shift is half-over, the kind where it's not yet clear if it was trending toward good or bad. Too soon to tell.

So, he thinks, too soon to tell what kind of day it was, let alone how the night would go. Or the rest of the week. Or the rest of her life. Any of our lives. Works in progress, out of our hands no matter how much we wish or pray or pretend to care either way. All these people holding on for the one thing no one was guaranteed, no matter how often they went to church or how many people they managed, no matter how big their houses or small their waistline: time. Only God, assuming he existed, could tell anyone, in advance, exactly how much time anyone had. Unless someone was willing to get in the way, preempt God's bigger plan. Someone, for instance, exactly like him.

Now's the time.

He repeats the words, loud enough that even *she* might hear them. Or could, if not for the sound of the bullet leaving the gun, hot to his touch, having baked inside his backpack on a High Alert Day. There's AC in the store, of course, but it would take a long time for his piece to cool down, especially after it's been fired. Most especially after it had been used until the clip was empty. He realizes he has one final choice to make. (*You're fired*, he thinks—head shot confirming this is the last time she'd ever sort of look at him, at anything—almost his last thoughts, his suicide note exploding in real time and living color. *Something to remember me by*, he thinks.) Actually, a few choices still need to be made: there are more people than he has bullets (he could have brought more ammo; he certainly had plenty, but that would have been too heavy to carry, and he'd never gone the extra mile at any point in his life, so why try impressing anyone, least of all himself, at this late stage?). He has to choose: who's in, who's out. He starts toward the produce aisle, all the way to the right, and realizes that's how everyone entered the store, where everyone begins. But this is a story about endings (*The End*, he thinks), so he heads in the opposite direction: cleaning supplies. *Clean up in Cleaning Supplies*, he thinks, smiling inwardly. He walks quickly, unable to hear the gasps and screams because the gun's still in his hand; it's simply not possible to hear human voices over the sound of hot lead exploding from steel, heading toward whatever luck or fate or random nothingness determined. He fires off a few rounds, mostly clean hits, but he won't be around to tally up his stats.

THIS KIND OF MAN

There's only one thing left on his mind at this point, as the seconds count down to the end of so many stories: *Make sure to save at least one for yourself.*

II

PHILIPPI

"There's a story here," she said.

I told her I didn't doubt it. "Each town has at least one or two stories behind it, right?"

"Well, I suppose that's true," she replied. "But most of them are never heard. It's the same ones that get told over and over."

I told her I'd never really looked at it that way before.

***

Jesi had a way of doing that. It seemed like she was constantly causing me to see things from a different perspective.

That's what immediately attracted me to her: She was unlike anyone I had ever dated, and that was good. She was, in fact, unlike just about anyone I'd ever known. Then again, she was the first person from West Virginia with whom I'd enjoyed more than casual acquaintance. We worked for the same law firm downtown in the bureaucratic honeycomb of the nation's capital, though our paths to arrive there diverged.

Indeed, our respective backgrounds could not have been more dissimilar. She had risen above the austere conditions of borderline poverty and indifference, the youngest—by many years—of four children. She had never known her mother, who passed away shortly after bringing her into the world. Her father's brother—a Baptist preacher and chronic drunk who'd never married—moved in as after her mother's death in what was supposed to be a mutually beneficial arrangement.

As for myself, I had always been an underachiever of sorts—a *late bloomer* as my mother optimistically referred to me when her friends inquired about her youngest son—and I would have been remiss to overlook the influence my father exerted in facilitating my somewhat coveted position at the firm.

Jesi was the first one in her family to attend college, and from what she expressed to me, financial support was not the only form of assistance she had lacked. Upon graduating, she had also been the first—and only—member of her family to leave West Virginia. Neither her father—whom, based upon her habit of referring to him in the past tense, I presumed was also deceased—nor her siblings had ever ventured outside a thirty-mile radius of their hometown of Philippi. In the time I'd spent with her, she'd been equally prone to castigate and endorse her birthplace with an almost admirable intensity.

One's hometown, it seems, is not unlike one's family in this regard: fair game for comment or critique, provided it's supplied by the individual who's invested in the experience and bears the scars. Similar sentiment, no matter how salient, from anyone else—an outsider—is seldom acceptable, and subject to reprisal.

THIS KIND OF MAN

Although I consider myself open to adventure and novel experiences, it was with some circumspection that I found myself accepting the invitation to accompany her to her ten-year high-school reunion.

Having grown up in the subdivided sprawl of northern Virginia, less than thirty miles from where the President lived, I had never really had the occasion, or inclination, to venture west—to the *other* state. It never actually occurred to me, until meeting Jesi, how tenuous and even discounted were the ties that bound our state to the silent one beside us that shared our name.

She remarked that West Virginians—if they allowed themselves to think about it in the first place—tended to regard my state with the type of jaded envy a younger sister might harbor toward the older sibling who received an unjust proportion of attention and opportunity. Ours was the one, it seemed, that had collected the dowry.

More so than any other state, West Virginia retains an insular, even inaccessible history and functionality. There is an aura that seems to entrench all of Appalachia which renders it detached and excluded from the imperative for itinerancy—that ever-present air of possibility, however illusory—which seems always to have informed the sensibility of our perennially rootless nation.

***

I recalled these things as we entered Philippi, a town that was not unlike every sentimental movie maker's depiction of a venerable place, long ago lost to time and memory.

"It isn't really a one-horse town," I offered facetiously. "It's more like a *half*-horse town!"

The quick glance this remark generated did not indicate anger so much as a wary exasperation.

"This is it," she exclaimed, looking around with excitement undercut by apprehension.

I gazed at the white sign she was pointing to, with its worn wording informing unenlightened passers-by like myself that the first land battle of the Civil War had been fought on this still-verdant soil. Immediately, I recollected that many of the prominent highways where I came from were named after the illustrious—and still exalted—Southern generals of that contentious campaign, and that it had never seemed especially anomalous to drive by a carefully preserved battlefield, surrounded on all sides by rows of new townhouses—unlikely armaments of brick and painted wood.

"This is what your state *used* to look like," she said, gesturing to the dense patches of trees that remained undiminished by the unobtrusive houses. Indeed, the paved roads seemed an almost inappropriate presence amidst the rounded, uneven hills and unrepaired fences splattered with mud and the impervious emblem of time.

"You'll notice that almost every front yard has its own satellite dish," she remarked, shaking her head, as we drove further out from the cohesive centrality of the town. "Most of these folks don't have a pot to piss in or a window to throw it out of, but they sure as hell have their television sets."

THIS KIND OF MAN

She drove us alongside the river, over an increasingly narrow road that appeared to have at some point been in the process of being paved, and then abandoned long before the project was near completion.

"I can't believe *this* place is still around," she said, pointing with an expression of surprise and approval at a long, white trailer that seemed to have taken root in the damp dirt. It was windowless and unadorned, except for the one word etched in broad black letters above the entrance.

"That's a *bar*?" I asked. "Is it for real?"

"Oh yes, it's real. My brothers used to go there all the time to get drunk and shoot pool."

"The place doesn't even seem big enough to have a pool table...it doesn't even look like it has electricity."

"I know...there aren't any kegs or anything, there isn't even an actual *bar*—just a bunch of stools and an old pool table. They serve beer by the can, or they used to, anyway."

"Have you ever been inside?"

She gave me a funny look. "Of course not."

"Really? Well do you want to go check it out?"

She told me it wasn't a good idea. "You wouldn't be very welcome in there," she said.

"Are you kidding?"

She wasn't. "The way you're dressed, you look...no, that wouldn't go over very well, at all."

I was somewhat taken aback. "Well, if that's the case, it sounds like I'm not going to *go over very well* this evening..."

She smiled. "No, you'll be fine. Most of the people who will be there tonight have at least been exposed to other things. They've actually been outside the town here."

I found that, despite my disappointment, I was nevertheless intrigued. The random possibilities I imagined occurring inside that peculiar bar at once fascinated and offended me.

"Well, we can check into the motel now, unless you want to drive around some more..."

I told her that I wouldn't object to more sightseeing. This seemed to be the answer she was hoping for, and I was relieved. It was, after all, her weekend. Her town.

"Do you want to go see the coal mine, the one you always tell me about?"

"Sure, we can go there, I guess," she said, without enthusiasm. "But there's actually someplace else I'd like to see first."

After a few minutes we crossed a one-lane, covered bridge, and turned off on a packed road which was like a dirt island, bordered by large mud puddles on either side. The sun's light, which had been seasonably warm, was all but obfuscated by the sunken shade of the brooding trees.

Eventually, this trail gave way to an immense, open field, and Jesi parked at the bottom of a hill strewn with jaundiced grass.

"It's up there," she said, pointing at the sloping maze of bushes and green clusters that sprang out from the tufts and mounds of baked brown earth.

"You mean we have to walk *through* all that?"

"Of course we do, don't be such a baby," she laughed, marching into the thick of waist-high overgrowth.

At the crest of the hill, in the center of a clearing, stood a decayed, one-room building that was, or at one time had been, a place of worship. The chipped white paint was cracking, and the front door either had fallen off or been removed by vandals. There was a circle of small, unadorned gray tombstones that surrounded the structure like a melancholy halo.

"This is my church," she said matter-of-factly.

I told her it looked as though it had been quite some time since anyone had celebrated mass here.

"I know, it's probably been ten years, maybe more."

Despite its neglect, the edifice retained a uniquely sanctified aura, occupying all the solitude and silence of a forgotten place.

Approaching the creaking altar, I was surprised to observe a large, wind-beaten bible still secure in its proper place at the pulpit, as though the final service had taken place and become suspended in time. I felt her walk up behind me and press against my back, gently grabbing my arm. "I want you to do something for me," she said softly, as if fearful of being overheard by an invisible assembly congregated before us.

"Sure, what is it?"

She told me.

I turned around abruptly. "Are you serious?"

She was.

"I've never been more serious about anything in my life," she said, putting her hands on me and closing her eyes.

It was as though we were at once insulated from any undesired detection and yet, there was an almost palpable presence I couldn't disregard. It seemed to me that our impulsive act had served to awaken all the eyes and ears that had ever gathered in the now dusty and disheveled pews.

Jesi seemed to not only sense something of this herself, but was actively and eagerly seeking to engage these strange, silent spectators.

She was loud. She spoke, saying things that made no sense, or that held no meaning to me: rehashed conversations and names of people who may have at one point belonged to this disbanded parish. It was difficult for me to concentrate, even with my eyes shut, because it was apparent she scarcely noticed my participation as she went about confronting, or defying the history of this church, and whatever significance it held to her.

***

The reunion was being held at the volunteer fire department, which had a modest banquet hall that clearly served as an all-purpose locale for the town's functions, ranging from wedding receptions to church bingo, to special occasions—like tonight. There were neither windows nor air conditioning, so the room retained a cozy, if slightly claustrophobic feel. Enough

THIS KIND OF MAN

cigarettes, cigars, and pipes had been enjoyed within its confines to leave the walls indelibly stained; the cinderblocks looked as if they might begin emitting tar at any moment. There were fold-up chairs and collapsible tables spread out in one of the corners. In short, it was exactly as I imagined it might be.

My own ten-year reunion was scheduled to take place later that year, and there had been over five hundred students in my graduating class. At this event, there couldn't have been more than fifty people in attendance, and that included dates.

Jesi had warned me that it would not be unlikely, or out-of-keeping with the prevailing practice of the town, that this function would be sans alcohol, so it was to my considerable relief—and I presume just about everyone else's—that a keg had been tapped before we arrived.

We walked in, and she was immediately recognized by several people.

"Hey Jezebel!"

I turned to her. "Jezebel?"

"Nobody's called me that in years," she said, with the slightest look of consternation.

"That's interesting," I mused. "I guess I'd just always assumed it was *Jessica*..."

"Yes, well, I changed it...I changed a lot of things when I left."

Before I had a chance to comment further, the man who had called out to her from across the room had made his way through the small crowd and now stood in front of us.

"Hi there! Long time no see," Jesi greeted him with a smile, embracing him warmly.

There was a buffet-style dinner, served in silver chafing dishes, and I wondered exactly how many celebratory affairs and formal functions had taken place in this room over the years.

There was music, dancing, and animated conversation. And much drinking. With a few exceptions—a handful of couples who still lived in town and saw one another regularly, and therefore content to leave before the event officially concluded—most of the people in attendance seemed perfectly intent to *tie one on*, an expression I heard repeatedly throughout the evening.

My own glass was never empty. The alcohol ameliorated my reticence and reluctance to unintentionally offend anyone—a concern that turned out to be unwarranted: the people I spoke with seemed genuinely interested in knowing who Jesi's *friend* was, and where it was exactly, he was from. For the most part, I stood off to the side, away from the locus of excitement my date generated. The primary topics of discussion involved marital and/or family status, locality, and, of course, the obligatory reminiscences of the good old days. Matters such as occupation and salary, if they were mentioned at all, were decidedly inconsequential.

Another factor, that I slowly understood undoubtedly contributed to the copious intake of alcohol by those in attendance, was the oppressive warmth in the room. Large, industrial fans stood in each corner, like set pieces from a silent movie, which only served the purpose of moving the air around in stagnant circles. Most of the men had quickly abandoned their coats, and several had already discarded their ties. Despite my discomfort, I remained unwilling to remove, or even loosen my own. It seemed that forsaking formality would lower my guard, or else be viewed as an overly ardent attempt to align myself with the solidarity of this small town. And, perhaps, some small part of my complacence resulted from a contentment to remain slightly aloof, and apart from the group.

As the evening wound down, those who remained congregated around the keg, and the room felt smaller and oddly secluded.

Jesi was becoming drunk. The geniality on display throughout the evening shifted to ebullience: She seemed increasingly incapable of expressing all the ideas and thoughts that were unfolding as her inhibitions continued to dissolve. It was as though she could not speak quickly enough, for fear of keeping up with what she wished to say, or that something might be left unspoken.

None of this provoked any noticeable disapproval from the group. If anything, they seemed refreshed, even seduced by her iridescence. I was certainly enthralled: She was radiating an exuberance that I had never been privy to.

We were given sufficient warning that the doors would be locked at midnight, in accordance with the agreed-upon conditions any occasion held in this building was subject to. This adherence to the inviolable conventions of tradition, which superseded the significance of any particular event, struck me as both refreshing and ridiculous.

Two couples joined Jesi and I in the parking lot, after transporting the dwindling keg that we now congregated around, like a campfire. I was pleased to observe that everyone seemed agreeable, and the conversation, like the beer, continued to flow freely. As one couple, who had relocated to the west coast, compared and contrasted their new place of residence, it occurred to me that I was the only remaining member of our group who had not grown up in Philippi.

Cognizant that I eventually needed to drive back to the motel, I had ceased drinking, and presumed it was the languid onset of sobriety that made the sudden change in Jesi so noticeable. She seemed distinctly unsettled, or nervous about something, and her speech, which had been loud and rapid, now seemed manic, infused with an urgency that made her slurred words difficult to comprehend.

Someone pulled out a pack of cigarettes, and I was surprised when Jesi requested one. She fumbled with it, unable to keep her hand steady as she grasped the book of matches, rolling the filter around in her lips. Finally, she succeeded in lighting it, and it promptly fell out of her mouth, extinguishing its decapitated flame as it bounced on the pavement. She squatted down to retrieve it, and then remained crouched, close to the ground, while we all watched her, amused yet concerned.

"I was raped," she said matter-of-factly, looking away as she scooped up the dead cigarette. No one said a word, the amiability at once sucked from the air.

THIS KIND OF MAN

"Do you know what that's like?" she asked, twirling the cigarette in her fingers, with the demeanor of a scientist observing some perfunctory data.

It seemed to me that her question was redundant, because it was obvious this was precisely what the rest of us were wondering, as we stood in muted disbelief. Each person probably wished to say something but was afraid of saying anything.

"I've had this...this *thing*, with me—all this time," she continued. "And you see, knowing what I knew, even when everyone else, all of *you*, thought I was this pristine little *child*..."

She paused, and I noticed that the looks on the others' faces—the ones who had grown up with her—were slightly distracted, and different from my own puzzled expression. I could not determine whether the shock of her pronouncement had created confusion as much as clarity—a confirmation of something that was beyond my comprehension. At once, the emancipating effects of the alcohol dissipated as the situation revealed its essence: It was—with the exception of me—once again a group of individuals who had been raised amongst one another in a homogeneous, if somewhat onerous, environment.

Everyone's eyes were fixed upon Jesi, who was looking straight up at the stars, either avoiding us or attempting to avert tears. No one spoke, and I realized that, probably for a different reason than the others, I was anxious for her to elaborate, and alleviate the excruciating silence she had caused.

Finally, she continued. "The thing about it is, I don't really mind, not anymore." She paused, letting the full effect of her words register. "I mean, not in the way you might think...I was young, and it wasn't...well, I didn't *know* any different." She stopped, looked up at us for a moment, then added: "I know that's not right...but it's the truth."

"Who was it, Jezebel?"

It was one of the men. I didn't notice which one of them had said it, I was staring too intently at her: her face, her mouth, and the astonishing words it had just calmly uttered.

"Jes...*who* was it?"

It was not so much a question as a demand. His tone was too loud, and choked, as though the words had needed to scale a considerable wall of bile to reach his tongue. Now the others were looking at him as well: It was apparent he already had an indication of whose name it was she wouldn't reveal.

"It was *him*, wasn't it?"

"It doesn't matter," Jesi responded, almost inaudibly.

She glowed. She seemed happy and relieved, as though finally shedding a mask that had long stifled her. It was odd; it was awful. Then she stopped, aware of herself and what she'd told us: It was as if she had forgotten how to breathe and was obliged to remind her body what was already, automatically, expected of it.

"Oh my God, I'm going to be sick," she gasped, standing up abruptly. At once, she was human again: pale and awkward as she stumbled into the darkness around the corner.

The two women followed her, leaving me with their husbands, who exchanged a slow, meaningful look I pretended not to notice.

THIS KIND OF MAN

"It was him," the one she had refused to answer hissed to the other. "It was that drunk bastard, that *priest*."

If it had not been sufficiently clear, it was now obvious that my presence—in light of this unexpected revelation—was no longer appreciated, or welcome. An outsider, I had intruded upon their insularity, making the situation that much more unavoidable, and unsettling.

"Christ, I think I'm gonna be sick too," the other one mumbled, quickly staggering up and away from us.

I shrugged my shoulders, in the hope of indicating that I understood, and it was okay. Or, if he preferred, that I didn't understand at all.

The two of us sat quietly, not speaking or looking at one another. The only sounds were the soft, interchangeable voices of the women around the corner. Finally, I sensed him staring at me, so I cautiously looked over.

"That priest," he said, glaring at me. Past me, really. "It was her uncle."

I shook my head, deciding it was best he didn't know I had already figured that much out on my own.

***

Later, after everyone was satisfied that Jesi was going to be all right, I drove us back to the motel.

"I'm sorry..." she began.

"No, it's okay, really..."

Fortunately, this seemed sufficient, and she laid her head back, shutting her eyes.

Once we arrived at our room, she immediately sprawled out on the bed, still wearing her dress and high heels.

I sat by the open window and watched the occasional, solitary truck speed by.

It was dark, but the stale heat lingered in the heavy air. Everything seemed unnaturally still, an almost conspiratorial silence, as though the town—its trees, its grass, its buildings—was wary of revealing secrets it continued to hold.

***

There was a picnic scheduled the following afternoon, and she asked me if I wanted to skip it.

"It doesn't matter to me," I lied. "We can do whatever *you* want to do."

To my considerable relief, she wanted to leave.

On our way out of town, we drove over a different bridge with different scenery than what we had encountered the day before. The unpaved road was exceptionally smooth, as though at some point a significant cycle of traffic had regularly passed over this route. Eventually, the thick space of trees gave way to a constructed clearing, and as soon as I saw the hulking, debilitated machinery, I understood where we were.

She didn't say anything by way of announcement or explanation, but it wasn't necessary. She pulled the car over and we sat silently, thinking our own thoughts.

THIS KIND OF MAN

The rusting pylons—whose emanations once signaled purpose and productivity—resembled the fossilized skeleton of an obsolete creature that perished in the obscurity of some prehistoric era. All around the mazes of water-stained steel the resilient, expansive landscape thrived: bushes and trees, which had been cleared away to facilitate the efficient industry of the men who mined this terrain, once again overwhelmed everything that stood beneath and beside them. The rocky banks that had been leveled and moved aside, after eroding and eventually resurrecting themselves with the persistent deposits of drifting dirt, formed a fortress around the defunct tunnels that enabled men to burrow into the ground for its lucrative spoils.

The mountain, which preceded and endured the coal mines, had ultimately reclaimed itself.

"How long has it been?" I asked.

She didn't respond for several seconds, but I could sense she was taken aback by my question, as though her thoughts had been transparent.

"I don't know, probably twenty years," she finally said.

This seemed to me very recent, and yet, to behold the relinquished apparatus, this once-thriving institution—and all that it signified—it seemed obsolescent, a shady artifact of an irretrievable past.

"The mines," she continued. "That's all they talked about. It was everything to them. They cursed it, feared it, *breathed* it. But mostly they loved it." She paused, then added: "The way you might love your family, I suppose."

I recalled the things I had read, and what she had occasionally related to me: the all-but incomprehensible adversity—incalculable hours spent in a dark space scarcely larger than your body; loss of weight from the heat in summer; frostbite in winter; black soot that seeped into your hair, eyes, ears, and lungs; the alcoholism; abuse and despair—that made this way of life so unique. So reciprocally repugnant and redemptory.

"When something becomes part of you, you can't imagine your life without it. Well, that's what these people had to do. It wasn't until it was taken away from them that they realized how much they actually had. *That's* the real tragedy of what happened here." She looked at me. "I can remember when this all started happening, you know. It seemed so unbelievable. Impossible, like the end of the world."

"Well, I guess it was," I offered. "At least in some regards."

"Yes, it was," she replied, turning back to the window. "I used to think that this place died, just stopped existing that year," she said, more to herself than to me. "Now it's like time simply stopped, and everyone forgot. The ones left behind, anyway." She shook her head slowly. "This town, this whole *place*, it will never recover." She looked at me again, and I saw she was struggling to keep herself from crying. "It's over."

I couldn't think of anything useful or relevant to say for a while. Then I finally asked a question I was sure she'd be able to answer.

"What happened? I mean, *why* did this happen?"

THIS KIND OF MAN

"I don't think there's a good reason," she responded. "I'm not even sure there *is* a reason. Whoever said that things had to happen for any particular reason?"

I thought about suggesting how most events, with the benefit and perspective of hindsight, usually revealed explanations that may not have been foreseeable, or coherent at the time that they occurred. As I tried to figure out a way to articulate this, I noticed she was no longer paying attention. I looked where she was looking: at the smoked-out silver pillars. They were silent, powerless. Humbled.

I wasn't sure exactly what prompted me to ask the question that unexpectedly sprang to my mind, particularly as I was suddenly sure that I knew the answer.

"Your father isn't really dead, is he Jesi?"

She glanced over at me coolly, and before I had the decency to look away, I watched her expression shift from surprise, to anger, then hurt—and finally—resignation.

"He's dead to *me*," she replied, making no attempt to disguise the hostility in her voice. "He's dead as far as I'm concerned."

***

As we drove out of town in silence, I figured out what had seemed so unsettling—and familiar—about the vacant coal mine, and the town itself: There was the conspicuous absence of commerce, the numbing influence of *man*. In the city—in any city—the asphalt and subdivided rows of buildings gradually attain an air of normalcy, supremacy: the city is a synthetic forest. But in the quiet and open expanse of an isolated place, God, it seems, is all around. The same God, perhaps, that had been overwhelmed, even annihilated by the skyscrapers and paved, sturdy efficiency of the city streets. Some places, perhaps many places, have not yet subdued the intransigent forces of nature, and God's reflection is still discernible in the sky and the soil.

Suddenly I felt compelled to make one more attempt, one more gesture of resolution.

"Listen Jesi, are you sure you don't want to go to the picnic?"

"Yes," she answered coldly. "I don't ever want to see any of those people...I don't ever want to see this *place,* ever again."

There wasn't much I could think to say. My inclination—which I kept to myself—was that she had gotten what she had hoped for, and perhaps more than she anticipated. In any event, I could sense the discomfort, her solemn resentment.

This had been her world; a world I still knew little about. A world she didn't seem to know anymore herself, for that matter. Either way, I found that if she didn't care to discuss it any further, as the car steadily put distance between the future and her past, I was not altogether unsatisfied with that arrangement.

THAT'S WHY GOD MADE MEN

It didn't get real bad, and my husband wouldn't even talk about it, until our son's senior year.

Another concussion, but we didn't call it that because that word wasn't allowed in our house. *He got his bell rung*, that's what my husband says. That's just how Jerry is, ever since I met him.

Our son, Jerry Jr., or J.J., is like his father in that way. Jerry is just like his father was, too. We always talk about how unfortunate it is that J.J. never got to meet his grandpa. Well, he met him, but he was too young to remember. We didn't take him to the funeral, either. Not because he was too young, but Jerry wouldn't allow it. He didn't even want me to go, on account of how shameful it all was. For him, for the family. What he did, Jerry said, it's just not something a man would do.

I know it's been hard on J.J., because he's always done things and Jerry will say, your grandpa would love that. But any time J.J. asks about him, Jerry gets angry, or won't want to talk about it. It's confusing, even for me, even after all these years. It's like we do talk about Jerry's father, and what happened, all the time, but we never really talk about it. I don't know, it's hard to explain.

The only time Jerry and me went more than a day without speaking was when I got fed up once and told him he was acting just like his father did. So I learned that's something I can't ever say to him.

I've always hated it when Jerry fights. I just don't like seeing people get beat up, even if they're asking for it. Like the most recent time, when that jerk stole our parking spot outside the grocery store. Even Jerry will say he hates violence, but that's why God made men. No one wants to get hurt or killed even, he says. God made men so things can get settled, otherwise it's all talking and crying, and that's what women are for. He knows that part gets under my skin, but it's what he always says. The world makes a mess and then men clean it up, he'll say.

Anyways, I hate how he gets so worked up that he always has to have the last word. When he comes home with a bloody nose or swollen eye I never even ask what happened. He'll just hold up his fist and say that guy started it, but *we* finished it. Like I said, I don't like it, but it's better than if he gets mad at J.J. or me.

Thank God for football. He always says that, too, and I agree. We met in high school when he was starting linebacker. He tells everyone he got varsity letters his sophomore year, but it was junior year; the same year I made varsity cheerleading. I sewed that #52 ribbon and Mrs. Kowalski told me to take it off. You're not Jerry's personal cheering section, she said. So I wore it on the inside of my uniform, me and Jerry's little secret.

It's funny, Mrs. Kowalski always seemed so old and crabby, but I bet she was younger than I am now. I know that's probably

THIS KIND OF MAN

the way all J.J.'s friends see me. They would never guess I was runner-up for Homecoming Queen.

But thank God for football, we say, because without it we may never have met. I would never have talked to such a pretty girl, Jerry says, but I don't believe that: all my friends had crushes on him. The truth is, I might not have talked to him either, he was so popular and all. That's why marriage is so special, the way you grow to love someone and see things you'd never notice when you're only a teenager.

And thank God for football because otherwise what would J.J. and his father talk about? I always say that to my friends, but I really wonder sometimes. Or if we'd had a daughter instead.

Like I said, J.J. is definitely definitely a chip off the old man's block. Even more so his grandfather's grandson. They have the same kind of humor, never taking things too serious. Except football, of course. What are you going to *talk* about, my mother said, when I told her Jerry asked me to marry him. She never understood that it's true, opposites really do attract. If it wasn't for you, Jerry always says, the only sound in our house would be the TV, but not like he's complaining.

Like right now, this kind of quiet. Everyone is quiet in a library because they're supposed to be, but, but everyone is quiet in a hospital because they're afraid. Afraid to say something bad or maybe hear something bad. Quiet because other people are also afraid, and nobody wants to bother anyone or make things worse than they already are.

I'm afraid to say anything to Jerry because I know he's really upset. I've never seen him like this, like he might run off or even start crying at any second. We've been to the hospital on account of J.J. so many times. How many broken bones or stitches or minor sorts of surgeries? J.J. spent more time with doctors than teachers, was Jerry's big joke. That's part of being a football mom, I always said. You never really think too much about it, because it's never anything that didn't happen before.

But this time it's different. I used to say I never worried about J.J. until he got old enough to drive. All those times he laid out on a football field, I felt like I was part of it, even though I was only watching. It's like when he was a baby, as long as he stayed in sight nothing too bad could ever happen. Once they start driving, though, you can't be there unless you go everywhere with them. But J.J. never caused any real problems. He took his football too serious to ever do anything ignorant, like some of his buddies did.

Pain is part of sports, I know. Not feeling pain runs in our family, Jerry says. I always say I can't understand how you can teach someone to be tough without hurting them. He says I say that because I'm not a man.

But my son's going to be okay. He had his seatbelt on. That shattered thumb would have ruined his football career, but everyone except Jerry knows J.J.'s playing days are behind him. Usually, he asks the doctors a bunch of questions, and compares whatever J.J. is in for against what he's had or seen himself. But when we got here tonight, he only repeated the same thing he said when we got the phone call: Tell me he's going to be okay.

The doctor said his vital signs all checked out, and that's all we needed to hear. But then the police officer said he needed to ask us some questions, and that got Jerry going again. Yes, we said, J.J. could drink too much sometimes. No, we weren't sure about the drug use anymore, it was on and off. We had to admit that sometimes he didn't make the best decisions, especially since he got cut from the team. Like any kid would do, especially someone who was like a famous athlete, at least in this town. It's been hard on everyone since he had to move back home.

But this wasn't the first time a doctor or police officer asked us some tough questions. We've just done the best we can, as a family. Maybe it's time for that big half-time speech, Jerry said. But then he got quiet instead of angry when the officer asked that last thing, and it made me more scared than I already was.

Do you think there's any reason your son would want to hurt himself, he said.

***

Football has been very good to our family. That's what we all said when J.J. got his scholarship. Like his daddy, he played linebacker, but also fullback. I go both ways, was his big joke. That's something his father would never say. There's certain things you don't even kid about, he said. I know Jerry's father would have thought it was funny. He was real quiet, too, but he sure could tell the best stories, and he'd laugh real loud even when he hadn't been drinking.

We still don't know why he did what he did. I don't think Jerry and his mother have ever talked about it. My sister-in-law, the last time she visited, said the word we *never* say in this house. Too much wine with the turkey, maybe, but she asked Jerry how he never could put the pieces together. All those empty bottles, she said. All the altercations he got in, all irritable over nothing or else ignoring everyone for weeks at a time.

I do all that stuff too, Jerry said, and you don't see me making my wife a widow. We didn't have depression in our day, he said. That's a new thing, like not being allowed to spank your kids.

I thought that was a good one, but then Jerry's sister said a bunch of other stuff, right in front of our son and everything. That was three years ago and we haven't seen her since. J.J.'s freshman year at college, the year before he decided to take some time off. We never say failed out because failure's a decision, Jerry says. We just need to figure out the next play, he said. One play can change a whole game, he told me. And J.J.'s life isn't even in the second quarter yet.

But it seems sometimes like it's Jerry's father that's sleeping in our son's room. I mean, at least with my husband, even when he's not saying anything, I know what he's thinking anyways. Don't look at me with that tone of voice, is one of his favorite sayings, but all I need to do is watch his face and I can tell if he's mad, or happy, or if he just needs to be left alone.

With J.J. I just can't tell. When he was younger, he couldn't keep anything from me, and I reckon that's how most boys are with their moms. Even if the father gets the final word, sons also listen to their moms. When J.J started playing football, it was more about pleasing Jerry, and I understand how that is; just like it was for Jerry and his father. Winning a game: that was the only thing that could make the old man talk and shut up at the same time, Jerry says. It's about the closest thing to him saying he loved his father.

Football was good for our family, like I said. All I ask is that you be the best player on the field, Jerry liked to joke. But it was funny, because J.J. always *was* the best player, and it seemed like all his teams could never lose. Even when he got to high school and they didn't win, each week it seemed like J.J. broke another record, or did something else to get in the paper, or caused a recruiter to call. Those were the greatest days, for all of us.

Even the concussions didn't seem so serious. We called those headaches when I was a kid, Jerry would say. Then when the team wouldn't let him suit up for a game one time, on account of the new school policy, Jerry about lost his mind. It's just as well your grandfather isn't here, he said. He would have stood on the fifty-yard line cussing at everyone, and they'd have to carry him away by his boots. J.J., just like his father, smiling and shaking his head, never allowing anyone to see any weakness.

Pain is just fear leaving the body—that's another one of Jerry's favorites. I know he would repeat things like that, especially when he coached Little League, to keep the kids motivated. Even I'd admit a lot of parents want try to pretend they can keep anything bad from ever happening. Life is also a game, but you don't get to wear a helmet, Jerry says.

The thing of it is, all this happened with his helmet on. Some people say these things keep happening *because* of the helmets. They say boys are so big and athletic these days, it would be safer without helmets and pads. But even Jerry talks sometimes about his father, a quarterback, and how he'd complain about feeling dizzy after games. Or that there was never enough aspirin for the way his head would hurt, like a faucet he couldn't turn off. When he's drinking or around his friends, Jerry will say stuff like I got my bell rung so much I thought I was a church. Or how he and the other kids would throw up on the sidelines. Playing through the pain is what separates the big boys from the little bitches, he always says. That's what the men in our family do, he says. If my father was here, you could ask him.

The doctors can confirm that J.J. had three official concussions during high school. Nobody is sure how many in college, even J.J. doesn't know. Jerry says college made our son soft, and only losers need excuses. He blames it on the doctors who prescribe too many painkillers, which leads to other things. But Jerry knows he drinks too much himself, just like his father did. Take away sports and beer, what's a man got left, he says.

***

Thank goodness for Sarah, J.J.'s girl. High school sweethearts, just like me and Jerry. I know J.J.'s been a lot to handle, so I'm grateful we have her. For all the coaches and so-called friends who showed their true colors, Sarah is family as far as I'm concerned. Maybe if she'd gone to the same college things could have worked out different. But she didn't have any scholarships,

THIS KIND OF MAN

so she's taking some classes here at the community college. And she's waitressing, just like I did before J.J. was born.

I know my son tells her things he won't tell anyone else, because she talks to me about it sometimes. She turned to me when they went through some tough spots, even before J.J. came back from college. And I know she's not real close with her own mother. I explained to her things I wish maybe someone had told me, mostly relationship stuff. Like, they don't mean anything by it if they get real quiet sometimes. Or scream at other cars on the highway, or get mad at the ballgame on TV. Men deal with their anger different, is all. I tell her, you think J.J.'s got a temper, you should see his father.

She's also told me things I'd never know. Things Jerry would never want to know. I wonder what he would say if he knew J.J. was taking pills to help him with his memory. That they told him to talk to someone about it, like a professional. If I talk to a shrink my dad would die of shame, he told her. Sarah said sometimes when J.J. is in the car he forgets where he's driving to, or in the grocery store he won't remember what he's shopping for. That this started all the way back in high school, and he lied about his symptoms in order to play those last games his senior year. Sarah told me he said it felt sometimes like his brain was being slow smoked, like barbeque.

I wish sometimes we knew this stuff before he went to college. I wish he could have talked about these things, but then I wonder what it would have been like at the dinner table every night. It was bad enough when the school wouldn't clear him to wrestle, on account of his last concussion. Jerry said it was for the better, because he didn't need anything else to mess him up for college ball. I told J.J. to put that energy into his homework, but he said mom we both know I didn't get that scholarship because of my smarts.

I know Sarah feels guilty she never said anything about the steroids. J.J. said all the players did stuff behind the coach's back, and some of the assistants even knew about it. J.J. said in college they won't let you practice if you're hurt, so you have to work out on your own. You do whatever you can to get back on the field. You have to have an edge, is what Jerry always says.

I know Sarah's parents don't approve of her and J.J.'s relationship. Her mother never did, at least since graduation, and for sure after that time when J.J. spent a night in jail. True, they were having one of their rough patches. But even Sarah would confess it was wrong of her to go on a date with the bartender from the restaurant she works at. One of J.J.'s good friends, or used to be, anyways. And no one's saying it was right what happened, but J.J. paid the price for what he did. Another man's woman, Jerry said. In our day that would have got laughed out of court. Fortunately, Jerry used to coach with the boy's father, and they worked it so lawyers didn't have to get involved.

They're going to take away his driver's license, at least for a while. The police officer said after the last time that if he messes up this bad again, no one's going to be able to pull any strings for him. I'll admit, it was hard those first months after college when he'd never leave the house. But now, after this, it's better if he stays safe and we know where he's at. Like he's a toddler again, I just won't let him out of my sight. It sounds like he may be in a wheelchair for a while, but we can handle that. Maybe Sarah can stay with us and help carry the load. Maybe this will bring them closer together. Maybe this will

THIS KIND OF MAN

bring Jerry closer to all of us. Maybe all this is happening for reasons we don't even understand.

As a parent you're supposed to do whatever you can to protect your child. I tell Jerry I would give anything to trade places with our son. Give me the headaches, the memory stuff, the depression, or whatever you want to call it. I'd go to prison if I had to, or spend thirty days in that facility we can't hardly afford. But I don't tell Jerry how scared I really am. That maybe our son won't ever get better. That he'll end up getting drunk all the time like his grandfather did. Or that he'll get in more fights or have another accident and mess up his brain even more. That maybe he'll really hurt someone one time, like Sarah, or me, or Jerry. Or himself. That one day he might look at me and not know who I am.

***

They're letting us see him now. Jerry told me and Sarah to go in together, that he'd let us go first and wait until later. Seeing two pretty ladies will cheer him up, Jerry said. But I don't think he's ready yet himself. I'm not sure Jerry is able to see his son like this.

Me, I can handle it. So long as he's alive. If he's alive, I can take anything. I saw him when he came into the world, all wet and helpless. I saw him when they took his tonsils out, tough enough to eat ice cream the same day. I saw him in the emergency room after he split his chin open. I saw him when they put his shoulder in a splint, using pins to hold it together.

I saw what happened to his hand when he punched our sliding glass door the day he came home from college. I saw him that last time, when they took him away in handcuffs. The kind of thing no mother should ever have to watch. I saw him cry the other night when he told me he'd never feel like himself again.

I reckon I can handle anything, as long as he's alive.

But I'm still afraid. It's not on account of what I'll see but what I might hear. I'm not worried about what the doctors will say, or even what I'll say because I'll say anything. I'm scared that my son is finally going to talk about things no one's prepared to hear. Some of the things men in our family have never been allowed to say.

RED STATE SEWER SIDE

It started right away.

The looks, which, by now, D.J. had come to expect. But this time, and from the moment he walked into the classroom, there was a hostility in some of their eyes—the girls as well as the boys—that he was unaccustomed to.

Still, he knew the drill. His third school in three years. He'd learned the routine the way anyone in his situation must: anticipate—even accept—the curiosity, the distrust, the time required to make a friend or two, eventually prove he was okay. Then, it was a gradual process of becoming assimilated.

In some ways, he'd discovered, being the new face amidst kids who'd mostly grown up together could be an advantage, especially with the girls. They were typically friendlier, even interested in who he was, where he'd come from.

And he had a story to tell. His father's job had taken them to three states in four years, something his mother called their "Apple-Asian Tour," whatever that meant.

My father's an *efficiency expert*, he would explain, even though he had no idea what his dad actually did. He knew it was something important, something that would impress. Even as a sixth grader, he understood you couldn't call yourself an expert; that's something other people called you.

He was, which he'd come to appreciate on some instinctive level, normal in all the required ways (not dumb, not *too* smart, able to go steady with the girls he liked), still too young to understand these were the ways males without paychecks measured themselves.

Cognizant of these things, he was disappointed when no one offered him a seat in the cafeteria. But he was not completely surprised. Somehow, his mother had predicted this. She was usually the one most excited about the next location, the *new adventure*, but this time it was different, and he'd noticed. When she noticed that he'd noticed, she tried to act the way she usually did, but it was too late and that made it worse.

"It might take a while longer," she said the night before. "These kids may not be quite what you're used to."

Unsatisfied, and vaguely unsettled, he asked her to explain.

"Well, there probably aren't a lot of new students each year, like at those other schools you've been to."

"Why not?"

"Well, I think most of these kids have known each other…they've lived here all their lives."

Isn't everywhere like that, he'd wanted to ask, but noticed again that she was acting different.

Before bed, he tried again with his father.

"Isn't that the way it would be for me if we'd never moved?"

THIS KIND OF MAN

"Just remember what we talked about," his dad said. "Be polite and don't look for any trouble. But don't be afraid to assert yourself."

His dad had never said anything like this, and it confused him. It made him want to talk about it more, ask questions he couldn't quite articulate. His father changed the subject.

"I wonder what kind of basketball team the high school has," he said.

As D.J.'s father stepped out of the shower that morning, he had seen his wife was already awake and dressed. She was worried.

"It's just business," he'd said, for the hundredth time, the night before.

"Thank god the unions are dying," he said, hanging the towel on the door.

"It's still going to be bad," she said.

"Yes. But layoffs are unavoidable, even at companies that have been around forever."

"I know, but here it's just...I mean, what else are these people going to *do*?"

"There's training, there are programs..."

"There's unemployment."

"Yes, there's always that."

The playground, at recess, was his chance, and D.J. was happy to take part in the football game. Basketball was his best sport, mostly due to his recent growth spurt, which his mother had called a "pre-empty strike on puberty," whatever that meant.

Somehow, his father had guessed the kids would favor football. Of course, basketball was more of a cold weather, indoor sport.

Still, he knew this was his opportunity to make an impression, to introduce himself, without words. It was touch football, but his classmates were rough, some of them coming at him particularly hard. No problem, he was prepared for that. But even when the action was elsewhere, they were relentless. There was one he identified right away as a problem; there was always one, every time. A smaller boy, aggressive, who kept shadowing him, making contact even after the plays. It was obvious he was the leader, and none of the kids were calling penalties, so D.J. started taking it to him. No choice but to give as good as he got, like his father always said to do.

It didn't work. The kid was tough, quick, determined. D.J. was used to being able to impose his will, using his size to his advantage. This kid kept coming back, his hands flying everywhere, way too close to D.J.'s face. He waited until the kid caught a pass, then tagged him up high, accidentally on purpose forcing him to the ground. The kid landed hard, but was immediately back on his feet, fists raised.

"Okay, you motherfucker," he hissed.

"Kick his ass, Breece!" someone shouted.

D.J. was taken aback, not only by the language (there were bad words, there were *bad* words, and then there were *off-limits* words), but the eagerness with which the other kids formed a circle.

"Not here, boys," the P.E. teacher said, walking over. "You'll settle this after school, if you want."

Again, D.J. was taken aback. While grateful for the intervention, it was the first time he'd ever heard a teacher condone, even encourage, a fight.

D.J.'s father had done his best to reassure his wife.

"You think growing up an Army brat was a picnic for me?"

"I know," she said.

"This is part of becoming a man," he said.

But he's not a man, she wanted to say.

"I know," she said.

"Plus, D.J. can hold his own."

"I know."

"And one thing is the same: boys will be boys, wherever they are."

"I know."

D.J.'s father had taught him the fundamentals of boxing, which had come in handy on a couple of occasions. But during the last year, being a few inches taller, refusing to be bullied, and simply being willing to stand up, had been enough.

This time was different, and he accepted it. Get it over with right up front, and then see which kids he'd be able to connect with. Heck, in third grade, he'd even become best friends with the kid he had to beat up.

Back in the classroom, he kept wondering how his parents had known: his father not wanting to talk about it, his mother talking about it too much. They knew, somehow, and he, of course, had picked up on it.

He'd gone to bed earlier than usual but was unable to fall asleep. First day jitters, same as usual. But still. He'd heard his parents talking, their whispered words easier to hear than if they'd been shouting.

"Yes, it's going to be a challenge for him," his father said. "It's going to be hard for all of us, for a while."

"I don't understand why everyone seems so angry," his mother said.

"Can you blame them, really? They keep electing idiots who make sure everything gets worse. What can you do with people like that?"

"The coal mines are never coming back, that's for sure."

"That's exactly what I spend my days talking about. Learn new skills, adapt. But nobody wants to listen."

"It's red state sewer side," his mother said, whatever that meant.

In D.J.'s experience, girls usually showed up at fights, which was a good chance to make another impression. Today, there was not a single girl amongst the dozen or so kids who walked outside after school, past the playground and toward the woods.

THIS KIND OF MAN

Suddenly, two other boys, either overly excited or with their own beef, started jawing at each other, then pushing. To D.J.'s amazement, within a few seconds they were rolling around in the dirt, a dust cloud of fists and curses. The scuffle was surprisingly intense and went on for what seemed a long time. He began to feel an odd relief; maybe this unexpected bout would offer distraction, if not get him off the hook.

But once the boys were separated, one of them wiping his nose on his muddy sleeve, D.J.'s adversary stepped forward. D.J. understood that what everyone had just witnessed was a warm-up for the main event.

Before every fight he'd been in, there was a sort of ritual: bravado, bold words, some shoving, and occasionally the opportunity for the other kid to back down.

"Get him, Breece," the boy who'd just won his scrap yelled, and D.J. stepped back from the oncoming barrage of punches.

Being taller, he used his jabs to keep the other boy away, able to handle his opponent without difficulty. But just as he'd seen at recess, the boy was wiry and relentless: he kept coming, and it took a lot to put him down. And he wouldn't stay down.

In D.J.'s experience, after a while—usually quickly—the other kid would want to shake hands, or say "uncle," or cry. This one, he understood, wouldn't be shaking hands or saying "uncle," and looked like he'd never shed a tear in his entire life. In fact, it appeared as though he was genuinely enjoying this.

It unnerved D.J., and even as he kept landing blows, he began to feel afraid. The faces all around him, at once eager and scornful, made it seem like someone might jump in at any moment. Then the P.E. teacher appeared, like before, as if by magic.

"Get 'em apart. You had enough, Breece? Look like he busted you up pretty good."

"Shit no," the boy said, hawking a mixture of snot and blood at D.J.'s feet. "I can take this fucker."

D.J. didn't have time to fully register—or process—his disbelief. The teacher simply nodded, and D.J. retreated into a defensive crouch to fend off another flurry.

On his way to the hospital, D.J.'s father avoided thinking about what awaited him by replaying what he'd just seen.

***

When he oversaw his first group layoff, the idea of armed security was ludicrous, like something out of a bad sci-fi movie. A great deal had changed during the last two decades, in his profession and everywhere else. Now, most offices had some type of security employed around the clock. Certain things remained the same, naturally. He had been called every name imaginable, been threatened, invited to step outside, spit on (twice—once by a man, once by a woman), and, on one memorable occasion, harassed at home—back in the days before caller ID and cell phones. And, unfortunately, he'd seen grown men cry, too many times to count.

Until today, however, he'd never seen a dismissed employee threaten to take his own life, on the spot.

THIS KIND OF MAN

"Of course we don't have metal detectors here," the shift manager said after, nonplussed but also slightly indignant. "How we gonna keep people bringing they guns? That's their *right*..."

It was unbelievable. It was almost as though this halfwit was defending the practice of packing heat, on the job, during working hours. No, he *was* defending it.

But this wasn't the worst thing. The man's swearing, surrendering his pistol, his uncontrollable bawling followed by a kind of furious begging, none of these were the worst. The worst wasn't even that the police officer knew the man—was clearly, on some level, friends with him, and kept calling him by an obvious nickname.

"It's okay, Cakes," and "It'll be all right, Cakes."

The worst thing was his suspicion, no *certainty*, that it was only his security badge—his status of being in charge of the people in charge—more than any laws, or customs, or unforeseeable circumstances, that ensured *he* wasn't the one being forced off the premises, and not on his feet either.

He had been comforted to get his wife's call, at first. After what he'd just seen go down, he needed to tell her, to talk about it with someone who might understand. Actually, with someone who definitely *wouldn't* understand. Just like him.

But then she said two things that confused and frightened him: *emergency room* and *bitten*.

***

Even here, he thought, as the young-looking (too young-looking) woman approached him in the parking lot.

"Excuse me, sir," she said softly.

He knew the script, had been hearing it more regularly: outside grocery stores, coffee shops, movie theaters, anywhere. Now, even hospitals. Typically, he had a dollar or two to give; it was the least he could do.

"I'm just trying to get something to eat, and…"

"It's okay," he said, handing her the first bill he pulled out. "I don't need the story. Here you go…"

The woman looked at him as though he were a god or some kind of alien, and then back at her hand, like she'd never held twenty dollars before.

In the elevator he repeated the short, unsettling conversation he'd had with his wife.

"Unconscious? How's D.J. going to get knocked out from being *bitten*?"

"No," his wife said, her voice unsteady with fear, but also something like awe. "After he bit him, the other boy kept punching him, over and over."

He looked down at his son and felt ill. Ill at what had happened. Ill at everything that would happen next, starting here in the hospital. And especially ill about the ragged wound on his son's cheek: the stitches it would require; all the possible infections attacking his system.

He felt ill.

THIS KIND OF MAN

"It was a fair fight," the P.E. teacher had apparently said, once the paramedics arrived.

Who teaches their kid to fight like that? To bite, like some rabid dog? And who knew what types of germs were in that boy's mouth, trapped between his teeth. Did that boy even brush his teeth? How often? And what was the quality of the meat his family ate?

How much do we become like the animals we feed on?

He looked at his son's bruised and beaten face, awake now but in another state altogether on account of the IV drip.

The surgeon had been speaking for some time, but he hadn't heard anything.

He was sick, with a sudden dread that the doctor was going to remove his mask and reveal himself as the man he'd just been paid to terminate. Or the one who'd similarly been escorted off another site the year before. Or a stranger he'd insulted at some point in his career, wherever his travels had taken him. Or maybe the nameless kid whose ass he'd kicked, behind another forgotten school. Or else—he imagined, as he half-fell, half-fainted into the reclining chair, at once toward and away from his son—some unfortunate soul who hadn't even been born yet.

SCARS

Jack can tell right away that Richard is already drunk. Good. Usually, they had to work up to it, one beer at a time. Or lately, in Richard's case, one vodka tonic, easy on the tonic, at a time. It just goes right to my gut, he said, when Jack finally asked what's with the pussy drinks. Beer just sits in your belly, Richard said. And it's not like I'm gonna jog it off, right? They both laughed.

There it was, distilled to its essence: a relationship primarily consisting of laughing and drinking. And sports, well, at least until that was no longer a possibility. Jack had long since stopped going to the gym and his outside shot was for shit anymore. Also, he'd learned, the only people who can jog on a regular basis are born into it, like an inheritance. Or else they're insane. Which is also like an inheritance, he thought one time, smiling to himself.

Apart from Richard, he was the funniest person he knew. Always had been. Being impartial, he knew he'd be able to make himself laugh even if he wasn't, you know, himself. Both of them class clowns, always getting in trouble, their popularity getting them right out of it. You play ball in high school you're like a made man in the mob, at least where they were from. Basketball was a big deal here. So was laughing, and drinking.

THIS KIND OF MAN

Probably like that anywhere else worth living, but Jack had never been anyplace else and wasn't especially looking to.

"How was work, honey," Richard says.

"I called in sick, actually."

"Allergies acting up?"

"Always are. I think I'm allergic to work."

Richard laughs, thank God. Last time they hung out, Jack found himself complaining about work, maybe a bit too much, and Richard had surprised him, saying how lucky he was. Must be nice, he'd said. Nice to have a job to hate.

But you don't *have* to work, Jack hadn't said. Would never say. But really, work is overrated, he would say, if he could. And not just to make himself feel better.

"The thing about hating something everyone else hates? It makes you normal."

When Richard had said that, Jack hadn't known how to respond, so he didn't.

I *do* hate my job, he could have said.

If you think I should be grateful because I hate my job like anyone else, to hell with being normal, he'd said. To himself.

"If I could trade places with you," he'd said, looking at his friend's wheelchair.

"You wouldn't," Richard said, laughing for both of them.

Truth was, he didn't remember any of it. The before and after, obviously, but the actual *thing*, what would actually be referred to, in court, as the scene of the crime? Nothing. Besides, his lawyer agreed that it was best to say as little as possible. Don't provide any detail until they ask for it, he said.

The first thing he saw, after impact and before the professionals arrived, was the blood. He'd never seen so much in his life, not even in a movie. When he saw it, everywhere—on his shirt, on the steering wheel, on the windshield, on Richard—he knew his friend was dead. Or, more specifically, that he had killed his friend. And then, this: how was *he* unhurt? Must be in shock, he thought, the way a zebra supposedly doesn't feel anything, even as the lion's teeth tighten around its neck. At least that's what he'd heard on some nature show one time. But no, he literally did not have a scratch, which made things much worse, when the extent of Richard's injuries were cataloged.

And then all the questions, few of which he could answer to anyone's satisfaction, then or now.

Why?

Why didn't his airbag work, and was that some kind of miracle, considering? Richard's did, and since the idiot wasn't wearing a seatbelt, as usual, it's hard to argue that this wasn't for the better, despite the damage it did. Maybe if he didn't have his feet on the dashboard, as always, Richard could have walked to the ambulance. Instead, his heels went through the windshield (at 200 miles per hour, they learned), like two tire irons. Since he wasn't buckled in, the airbag bounced him back into his seat, and then forward, shattering his nose against his knees (that's where most of the blood came from). To add insult to injury, or *injury* to injury, Richard thought he'd been blinded

("I can't see!" he kept screaming), but it was on account of the chemicals the airbag released. They would later hear all about airbags, how they operate (or don't, in some cases), along with too-detailed descriptions of femurs, pelvises, fibulas, deviated septums, thermal burns, and partial paralysis.

How?

Not a tree, or a utility pole, or another car, but a deer. It wasn't uncommon; deer were everywhere, especially at night, especially that time of year. But still, what were the chances? Jack never saw it. But those fuckers are fast, he knew, from all the times he and Richard had hunted them, mostly never seeing one, and only on occasion getting a successful shot off. After all these years, he finally had his mounted trophy, a heap of fur and guts and broken bones on the hood of his car. Richard slumped forward, high fiving a hoof: like a sick reenactment of that famous painting of the creation by Michelangelo.

Where?

Where were we going? Home. Where the hell else do you go after the bar serves last call?

"How'd the date go?" Richard asks.

"Eh, it was okay."

"Did you close the deal?"

"Nah, she said she had to be up early, blah blah blah…"

"What about next time?"

"We'll see. I'm not sure I'm feeling it."

This was not the truth. He *did* close the deal, but it was best, Jack had learned, to parcel out good news or details of any conquests in careful doses. Out of consideration, obviously, but also for selfish reasons. Conversations between them were like maintaining a buzz: too much in either direction could derail everything.

"So what's up with the bandage?" Richard asks, motioning to Jack's hand. "Any other damage?"

"Nope. Not for me, anyway. It was just one punch, no big thing."

"Anyone I know?"

"Maybe. You remember Scotty Hanrahan? Was classmates with my kid brother?"

"Football player, right?"

"I guess so. He's fat now. Fatter than you even."

"Ha, ha. So, what happened?"

"We were actually just shooting the breeze, but he ended up getting all hammered. Started talking shit about the state finals, wouldn't shut the fuck up about it."

"What'd he say?"

"You know, the usual stuff. You were all a bunch of chokers. How's anyone gonna miss *two* free throws with a chance to win the game, chance of a lifetime, all that crap."

"So you popped him?"

"Yeah. I finally asked if he wanted to talk about it outside, and he did. Big mistake on his part."

"Good for you. Think you'll run into him again?"

"Who cares?"

"Wish I could have been there."

THIS KIND OF MAN

"Me too, man."

They got in their fair share of beefs, back in the day. Back when everyone knew them as Ricky and Jackie. Point guard and small forward, respectively: partners in crime, shared locker, double dates, equal opportunity brawlers. Never seemed like anything to question: life happened at speed, and you got laid, laughed, and won as much as you could. It all makes sense until one day, it doesn't.

The truth was, Jack hadn't been in a fight for years. Since before the accident. It wasn't that he didn't go looking for them anymore, so much as they didn't come looking for him. Only chumps go out of their way to stir the pot, but only cowards back down if the situation presents itself. It's a younger man's game anyway, which is something most guys figure out. The older you are, the more you have to lose. The more it hurts, the less fun it is.

The truth was, a fight *did* come looking for him the other night, but it didn't happen. It could have. In fact, Jack had welcomed it. Everything he'd told Richard was more or less accurate. That prick *had* been there and he *did* start popping off about the game. About how Richard missed those free throws, asking how that felt, that maybe his buddy deserved to be handicapped, and Jack *had* asked him if he cared to continue the conversation outside.

"Seriously?"

And when that asshole smirked at him, Jack had been ready to go, right there in the bar. But he froze up. For the first time in his life, he realized he was being laughed at. And then other people, bystanders who hadn't even bothered to stand up, also started laughing. It was something he wasn't prepared for. Something he could not have possibly prepared himself for. Every other time, instinct took over and he was busy inflicting damage before anyone could say another word. He was accustomed to other people backing down; being willing to throw down was half the battle to begin with. But this time the other guy wasn't declining so much as dismissing, acting not out of fear, but pity. Jack hesitated, then found himself walking away—faster than he would have liked.

Before driving home, and after busting his hand on the driver's side door, he understood it was over, his days of fighting were finished. Sure, he was older, and yes, he'd put on weight, and of course, he hadn't thrown a punch in forever, but there were all kinds of grown men willing to sort things out when they had to. And it occurred to him: the next time he fought, in a public place, he would *be* one of those men. A bigger, broke down version of who once was, a source of drunken entertainment for amused (or worse, embarrassed) spectators. And then it would become part of the program, expected even. Another adventure, another thing to bullshit about over beers, when buddies get together to retell stories and compare scars.

"So, any chance you'll change your mind about the wedding?"

Jack finally asks the question he already knows the answer to, for lack of anything else to say. Even though he knows it's best not to talk about it. He can't help himself; however uncomfortable their conversations could become, they were still better than the silence: Sitting there, staring at everything but one another, avoiding all the things they could never talk honestly about.

"I don't think so."

"I know the fellas would love to see you…"

"I know."

"And of course my brother told me to tell you…"

"I know."

"Anyway, this shit's expensive, you know? Renting a tuxedo, getting a gift. It's even a cash bar, can you believe that?"

"Well, your brother's smart. Or his father-in-law is anyway. Knows how much y'all drink."

"I'll need to be drunk for the toast. Getting up there in front of everyone?"

"Maybe I'll have to do that for you some day."

"Yeah man, I hope so."

There's an intolerably long silence.

"Need more ice?" Jack finally offers.

"Nah, just fill me up if you would. I'll drink it as is."

Jack does as he's asked, wincing inwardly. Warm vodka was a whole other level, he thinks. Still, it's better than silence. But not by much.

The thing about these silences, they weren't necessarily *silent*. Jack would still hear their voices. The things he said, to himself. The things they might say, to each other. The things they would never say.

I'm sorry, he'd like to say.

Don't say that, Richard would reply.

I did this to you.

No you didn't.

I did this to *us*.

No.

It should have been me.

But it wasn't.

I'm just saying, it *could* have been me.

But it wasn't.

I'm just saying.

Eventually, Richard's mother would come check on them. Maybe even offer them fresh drinks. She hated how much her son drank, but what could she do? Richard needed her and, with her husband gone (what a year *that* had been, dealing with that and then *this*), she'd come to rely on him as well. As Richard had adjusted to being dependent, she had readjusted to once again being his caretaker.

It had never gotten better between them: Jack always sensed how uneasy she was around him, and he accepted that. He knew she blamed him, and he understood. How could she not? Jack knew she also blamed her son. For being so reckless. And then shutting himself up in their house, refusing to see almost everyone. For not turning to his faith to assist him through this ordeal. For forcing her to confront the fact that there'd be no one for her when she got too old to take care of herself. And mostly for the amount of money they might have received, in addition to the insurance payout, if Richard had agreed to press charges against his best friend.

Okay, Jack thinks. I'm drunk, too. Finally. This is usually his opportunity to leave, his excuse for excusing himself. What was Richard going to say, have one more for the road? But the thing is, Jack *does* want one more for the road. Maybe more than one.

"I think my mom bought more beer. There should be some in the refrigerator."

"You read my mind," Jack says.

"Well…you want *me* to get it?"

"No, I'll go. Let me get another swig of that vodka first."

"Okay," Jack says, after a few more beers and swigs of vodka. "Let's each confess something we've never told anyone before."

Richard frowns, but nods his head. "You first."

"This is crazy," Jack begins "There's a dream, the same one, that I have all the time lately. Want to hear about it?"

"Why not."

"Well, somehow I've been cast in the high school musical. I know, right? Me, never acted a day in my life, in a play with all those freaks we used to make fun of!"

"So you're saying you're secretly a queer?"

"Ha, ha. But check it out. I've got the part, an important one, and the show's about to start except I don't know any of my lines. The fuck's *that* all about?"

"Pretty weird."

"The thing is, I always wake up scared. You know, like it really happened or something."

"Like it really mattered."

"Exactly."

They finish their drinks in silence.

"So," Jack finally says. "How about you?"

Richard opens a beer and studies it, like maybe it will speak for him.

"I still think about it all the time," he eventually says.

For lack of other options, Jack looks up and meets his friend's eyes.

"I mean, I replay it. Each thing, every detail. What I could have done different. How I'd do it over, today."

Despite himself, Jack is surprised, yet mostly relieved that Richard is finally talking about it.

"It's like, I can never get past it. I can't forgive myself."

"But," Jack finally says. "That's not on you. You have nothing to be forgiven for…"

"How do you figure? *I'm* the one who blew those free throws. No one else lost our chance to win states that night."

"But…it was just a game," Jack says after a while. Once again surprised and relieved. It was still easier for Richard to talk about the blown game than his ruined life.

THIS KIND OF MAN

It's true, Jack thinks, tossing the empty can out his window. I've always been the lucky one.

"It could have been me," he'd said, again. After his friend had smashed the vodka bottle. After he screamed at his mother to leave them alone. After, continuing the same conversation that seemed to have started before they were born, Richard allowed Jack to talk about it.

"But it wasn't you," Richard said, refusing to look at him.

"I'm just saying…"

"It wasn't you who got his legs messed up that night. Just like it wasn't you who missed those free throws. Maybe you would have choked too, but you didn't. Just like it wasn't you whose girl dumped him the night before prom. Remember? How we reserved that hotel room? The limo? By the way, that was bullshit you never gave me my money back. You shouldn't have made me pay for half."

"I'm sorry," he'd said.

"Just like it's *never* you. Every girl, every fight. Every game. Everything."

I did lose that night, he could have said. You called shotgun first, so I had to drive. Same rules as always.

"You've always been the lucky one," Richard said.

We drove drunk all the time, he could have insisted. And you should have been wearing your seatbelt. And you always would put your feet on the dashboard, just to annoy me.

He could have said these things. Or he could have told his friend about the other dream he repeatedly had. The one where he eventually notices the lights behind him, and it's not concern he feels so much as relief. This *had* to happen, he thinks, as they cuff his hands behind his back. This had, in fact, already happened. But this time they were going to make sure he remembered it. *Sometimes it takes something like this*, he understands. *Something to intervene. Save you from yourself.* And a feeling he'd buried deep inside his brain would start to shake itself free. Something that might, somehow, make everything different. Then he'd wake up.

He feels the autumn air on his face, and nods in approval. Football weather. Almost basketball season. Hunting, too.

Watch out for deer, he thinks, smiling to himself.

IN MY CUPS

When you're not certain where your next meal is coming from, and don't know if you'll be sleeping indoors ever again, there's one thing you learn to count on: coffee.

Let me tell you about coffee.

I've had free coffee and I've had coffee I paid for the way people buy used cars: slowly, agonizingly, counting the amount over and over, angling for a deal, hoping for an impasse, seeing a blank face staring back at me. I've paid a price for every cup of coffee that's ever crossed my lips.

I've had cold coffee and I've had coffee so hot it turned my tongue into a blistered sponge. I've had coffee that's sat in a stained thermos so long it smelled like an animal. I've had coffee so fresh it's turned me into an alien without words to describe it. I've had coffee when it's been so long between each cup that it tasted like the glistening drops from Christ's cross.

I've had coffee over conversation. I've had countless cups of coffee alone, composing symphonies of silence, epic poems of regret, confessions even I don't believe. I've bought coffee and I've brought coffee to someone who needed it even more than I did, feeling like an angel with dark stains under unclipped fingernails, glowing with a mercy I, too, hope to receive.

I've fought over coffee, holding the scalding prize with bruised hands. I've tossed a perfectly made cup of coffee into the street, some kind of statement to whomever is saying something I can't hear inside their air-conditioned cab.

I've dreamt of coffee, and I've woken up wanting coffee, like a scared baby grasping in the dark. I've spent entire afternoons counting the seconds until a cup of coffee will warm my extremities, even if it's an illusion. I've wondered if there's more coffee than blood streaming through my veins, like I'm some legless pedestrians and it's nothing but caffeine pushing me through these crosswalks.

I've crushed empty cups of coffee like the metal teeth of a trash compactor, ready for the next pile of whatever gets thrown at me. I've cursed coffee and wished to kill the people who give it away, or sell it, or use it as credit for a debt that can't be repaid.

I've seen and studied the ways coffee can buy compliance, a bribe, or an excuse.

I've imagined a world without coffee and people who don't care. I've caught myself creating a life where no one needs coffee because no one works, or looks for work, or has to pay for the things work provides.

I've had cups of coffee where I've counted how many cups it would cost to sleep one night in the cheapest motel. Or how many of those cups it would take to add up to a month's rent in the smallest studio in the most broken-down walk-up in this city. I've multiplied those cups to make a down payment on an apartment. I've sold it and escaped to some subdivision named after a tree they create in laboratories to grow faster and mingle well with other trees, lined up like fences, around houses,

THIS KIND OF MAN

around people who don't really know what hunger or heat is, or how time's only kept on clocks if you're leaving and arriving at a place you recognize.

And I promise myself it's not too late and it's never too cold, and one day I'll know what it's like to forget what it felt like. When the only thing I wanted was to be certain that I could reach out my hand and someone would meet me with a cup of what keeps me alive.

NO TENGO A NADIE

He runs.

He's made the mistake of walking alone near the junkyard, after sunset, and come upon the dogs. Usually, a deftly thrown rock or self-assured shout will discourage them, but this time the lateness of the day lends desperation to their enterprise. Or, perhaps, like the bigger boys who tormented him, these predators sense he's weaker, and easier game. Two things, he knows, will save him: his speed, and his awareness that they tended to tire—and lose interest—almost immediately. The solidarity of the pack was not sufficient; they were, he understands, at heart craven and without will.

(Always, he's has been running. He ran with pleasure as a child, faster than the others, his speed compensating for the brawn he lacked. He ran in his bare feet through the sharp, sun-scorched grass and the dusty red dirt, always familiar and warm, pulsating and alive on his skin.

Later, he ran to avoid pain. As he grew older, *peligro* presented itself in so many semblances it was impossible to confront head on. It was wiser, and safer, to learn quickly the necessity of running *from* things instead of toward them. Sometimes he ran from the other boys, who knew he had no

THIS KIND OF MAN

older brother to protect him; other times he ran from his father who, he knew, was simply transferring the aggression and frustrations that were siphoned onto him out in the coffee fields, where fists ended disputes and settled grievances.

He ran and would fancy himself running, over the hills of his countryside, away from the shacks and the unhappy adults tending their land—away from everything.)

He runs, but the dogs keep pace, drawing close enough that he can feel the dampness of their muzzles. As he glances over his shoulder, the dogs seem to smile, their bared teeth dropping saliva on the sand. For the first time, his fear is supplanted by a different, not unpleasant ambivalence. To stop running equals death, but does it not also mean freedom? *Too late,* he thinks as he's dragged down, among and between them.

***

He wakes from this familiar dream with pain: the sharp stabs in his feet, the sluggish pressure on his back, the cumbersome burden of his body. Sometimes, when he's unable to sleep, he utilizes the bottle that waits beside his bed, like a well-read bible. This elixir induces a fitful slumber which he pays for the following morning. That's his routine when, even after fourteen hours standing in one spot, his body screams for oblivion but his mind won't oblige, twisting around itself with thoughts and worries. He's afraid of everyone because he's unable to entirely trust anybody. He has always found it best to go his own way, and he's content to trust silence as his strength. But sometimes this is not enough, not in *los Estados Unidos.*

The first fear, of course, involves the papers: an ID, a social security number. These things can be arranged, *must* be arranged. All taken care of by other people whom you do not need to know. You *do* need to know someone who can help negotiate with these people, all of whom operate underground. No promises are given, only the knowledge that others have come before you, gotten what they needed. Then, one day a green card appears. To the untrained or unsuspecting eye, it all looks *auténtico*, a license to work anywhere they're willing to hire you. Many of these wizards make their livings exclusively from this practice, resulting in a product that's efficient and effective. And expensive. The amount a successful transaction costs is unimaginable, out of the realm of reasonable possibility. Nevertheless, you find a way to secure the resources, aware it means the difference between a decent job and picking strawberries in a sweltering field for $2.50 an hour, or whatever the *hijo de puta* can get away with paying. (Washing dishes, for instance, is a good job, particularly considering the alternative options, such as the uncertainties involved with construction work, or moving furniture, or washing windows two hundred feet above the ground—all outdoors, all day, in summer and winter).

With your *papeles* you have no voice and you are no one. Without them you are less than that.

Two jobs, the same job. The same work at two workplaces. A necessary and normal routine, because none of the employers are interested in paying overtime. The better jobs, in the better restaurants (where they provide you with plastic gloves, apron and a free meal each shift) do not come easily. Even if you're fortunate enough to find one, or make the connections necessary to get considered for one, there's always the fear of being replaced: you are easily expendable since the supply often outweighs the demand. So you work.

The day he became dizzy after sweating through two shirts and began coughing up the congealed phlegm in his chest (one was constantly battling head colds and flu-bugs, among the variety of ailments so easily exchanged in a restaurant, particularly when handling contaminated utensils and dishes) he swallowed aspirin until convincing himself the fever had subsided. Or the time he cut his fingers while attempting to unclog the drain (an incident that might have resulted in legitimate compensation if he'd the interest or inclination to pursue it, which he did not), he was obliged to wrap both hands, like a boxer, before putting on his industrial strength gloves to ensure that the highly concentrated cleaning solutions didn't seep into his sores.

He even washes dishes while he sleeps.

Of all the dreams, this one is most persistent: struggling to keep pace, he hears the clatter of plates being stacked, one pile atop another, and the harsh voices of the *pendejo* waiters, who relentlessly bring armful after armful, cursing him for moving too slowly. The faster he works, the more there is, impossibly, each time he turns around. *Mas.* Always, *mas.*

Or else he's vexed by recurring memories of the random brutalities he'd grown too accustomed to witnessing in his country. Frequently, it is the singular image of a face disappearing in an explosion of gunfire. Sometimes this face is his wife's, or his son's. Mostly it's no one in particular. Just another face.

***

He runs.

This time it's *los negros*. When the weather turns warm and the nights longer, there are usually clusters of them huddled under the streetlights of his apartment complex. But sometimes they lurk, under cover of the summer evening, and appear, shouting scornful threats—words he may not know, but always understands.

Give me some money motherfucker.

Usually, the older ones just laugh, and are content to insult him. He's much warier—and afraid—of the young ones, the *delinquentes*, because like the wild dogs, they came at you in packs, brazen when they outnumbered you. Then it becomes dangerous. So he runs.

Despite standing for so long all day, every day, he's still quick. But with his sodden boots and greasy pants he seems to move at half-speed. It's nothing more than the genuine, familiar fear of being caught—just as it was when he was a boy—that saves him.

***

From his cramped corner in the sweltering kitchen, he grabs another steel pan—the same one might get scrubbed clean

THIS KIND OF MAN

thirty times in a single evening—and gently places it in the sanitizing solution, always a numbing sensation after the steaming mess of filthy water. It doesn't take long for the feeling to leave your hands if you leave them long enough in the cold water, as he discovered once while emptying a drain clogged with broken glass. He didn't feel a thing until he pulled his shredded hands out into the warm air and saw the blood bubbling through the holes in his rubber gloves.

The waiters come and go, dropping off stacks of plates and then disappearing again, never showing a drop of sweat or a stain on their starched shirts. He catches himself gazing at their stylish black shoes, then down at his own, which are soaked, as usual, from standing all evening in a puddle that collects overflowing water from the oil-slicked sink. He feels it coming and shuts his eyes, resisting the vision that rolls familiarly, inexorably into his mind:

Someday he's a different man. He is jefe, *not* empleado, *smoking an expensive cigar at the end of each evening. He no longer wears work boots, only soft leather shoes without laces. He communicates freely and easily, no longer an* extranjero, *a scared stranger forever on the outside: outside time, outside himself. He asks for nothing because finally, for once, he needs no one.*

Then, as quickly as it came, the reverie is over. He opens his eyes and watches it slip into the steam rising from the scalding sink.

He doesn't understand, or exert any effort attempting to make sense of, the money removed from his paychecks every other week. Taxes, he knows, are neither fair nor unfair—they simply *are*. He is oblivious, or indifferent to the fact that the waiters, who make more than three times his salary, manage to pay almost none of the taxes.

He does understand, and is grateful for, the air conditioning that comes without question, like a door or a toilet, with each workplace. This is one of the miracles of the new country that one needed to experience in order to appreciate. Of course, there's little comfort in the oppressive air of the kitchen; but simply knowing this frigid relief exists makes it easy—and imperative—to remember a world without such wonders.

He doesn't understand how the towering wooden poles, standing guard over every street, are capable of harnessing and generating such impossible energy. This invisible mystery—providing light and power, and able to transport peoples' voices from one place to the next—represents a crucible of communication that's impenetrable and, for him, inaccessible. He does not question this.

He understands that in America, for him, Monday equals Tuesday equals Wednesday equals Thursday equals Friday equals Saturday.

He understands—and it didn't take long for him to realize—that here, appearance counts for so much. It's everything. Like money and muscle, it's power, serving to separate those that have it, from those who do not. The waiters are a constant reminder of this: all thin, clean, with perfect white teeth. If there's occasion for interaction, none of them—even the usually affable ones—can completely conceal their mostly vague, sometimes palpable, discomfort. When they

THIS KIND OF MAN

shake his hand, they do so lightly, rarely looking him in the eye. They never stand too close to him, as they do amongst each other. The *gringas* especially, always smiling and talking loud and slow, the way one would speak with a small child. Further, they seem keenly aware of their bodies and proceed cautiously around the kitchen staff, *the back of the house*, as they're all called. At these times he is conscious of himself, and the knowledge that he's not an attractive man. Ill-luck, circumstance, and the strains of life have conspired to make him appear older than he is. The choices he's forced himself to make have given him the chance for a real life, but in return have robbed him of his youth.

And, above all, he understands this: *No tengo a nadie*—I have no one.

***

He sees himself in the darkness, high above the ground, alone on a decaying ladder, looking unsteadily below at the splintered rungs which spiral away and out of sight. He is afraid to look up, but as time passes his eyes grow accustomed to a feeble light that illuminates the commotion below: He can discern distant shapes climbing toward him—a cacophony of voices. As he stares, the shapes slowly become solid figures and he can eventually identify their shaded faces, mouths opening and shutting in a synchronous signal. They quickly cut the distance, moving with vigor as they spot him—thousands upon thousands filling the space and creating a bulwark between him and the nothingness below. Unnerved, he scales the ladder, but in the shuffle, he slips as a hand reaches up and grabs his foot.

He looks down at the face, a face he recognizes and suddenly fears: He fears it will speak and he knows what it will say. Impulsively, he secures his grip and brings his boot down forcefully, watching as the body drops away, disappearing into the darkness.

***

    He's never seen blood like that, not even the time the chef was chopping veal shanks and cut clean through the bone of his finger. It was all but inevitable—your environment consisting of water, soap, grease, wet food, and a soaked floor—that at some point an accident would occur. It didn't have to be anything as dramatic as an errant knife, or a scalding pot touched with bare hands. It could be as random as what just happened to him: a broken beer bottle slicing through the trash bag being carried to the dumpster, following gravity and bad luck to a vein in the palm of your blistered hand. A chef, of course, can still work in a limited role while his bandaged finger heals. Or, if need be, he can take the time off—with pay—until he's able to resume control of his kitchen. This is a luxury not available to the dishwasher, who necessarily has his hands almost ceaselessly submerged in water. The dishwasher is expendable for all the reasons the chef is not. This is why he'd actually cried; not because of the pain, but the dread that this mishap would result in the loss of his job, just as it had been another's misfortune that expedited his current position. He insisted that if they wrapped a plastic bag around his wrist with electrical tape, he'd be able to continue. But even before arriving at the emergency room he was lightheaded from the blood he'd

THIS KIND OF MAN

already lost. As the shock began to wear off, the real pain started to settle in, like heavy clouds following a flash of lightning.

***

He's scared.

He opens his eyes and looks down at the same bloodstained clothes he left the hospital wearing. He's remained motionless on the bed, drifting in and out of a torpid slumber, alternately sweating and shivering. It might only have been a few moments since he'd put his head down. Or it could have been hours, or days. He reaches over for his bottle and sees it's empty, although he doesn't recall touching it, and doesn't feel the usual sluggish buzz. This is bad. The large white tablets, which are supposed to get him through the week, are already half-gone. His body feels heavy and warm, detached from him. But the pain, temporarily subdued by the medicine, is hovering around his hand, waiting, like a thief on the other side of the door. Suddenly cold, he pulls the damp blanket around himself and remembers the first time he saw the snow.

It was nothing at all like he'd expected.

He'd heard how parts of *los Estados Unidos* got frigid enough to make the rain turn soft and white, so he greatly anticipated this minor miracle the day the clouds finally hovered heavy and close. He'd sat at his window for over an hour, enraptured by the trees and ground slowly becoming smaller, gradually disappearing. After a while he ventured outside, half-expecting the glistening powder to support his weight.

Almost immediately his feet were sodden and the snow swirled around his face in broken sheets of blankness. He ran blindly, eventually stopping beneath a utility line, its wires humming in the darkness above. Whether on account of the crowded air or the disorienting effects of the storm, this edifice, which had inspired such awe, seemed somehow less spectacular to him now. With its mighty, metallic arms stretched to their limits on either side, it more than slightly resembled a resigned man, not the impervious instrument of his design. The power of this machine, with all its churning electricity, was something he feared; it was nothing he wanted any greater intimacy with. Neither the burden of its pain nor the profits of its oppression were his. Calmed by this cognizance, he retraced his steps back toward the shelter he'd never until now considered his home.

***

Once again running.

But this time there are no dogs, no strangers, nothing. There's no one following him, somehow. As he runs, he begins to sense a certain, strange weightlessness he's never known. He realizes he's wearing no boots: his feet are bare, like they always used to be, feeling the warm soil between his toes.

He runs, not afraid, not in danger; there is, for once, no *peligro*. Neither toward nor away from anything. He runs because he's warm and weightless, and this moment won't end if he doesn't stop running. He doesn't want to stop, so he continues on, weightless and warm.

He runs.

A BRIEF CATALOG OF MOSTLY FORGIVABLE THOUGHTS

Mostly, he thinks.

Watching his daughter—part angel, part human, part shark—attacking his wife's distended breast with something more like fury than hunger. More greed than desire.

After he thinks all the obligatory (and true!) thoughts about how beautiful everything is (how beautiful the baby is, how beautiful his wife is, how beautiful this act is, how beautiful the world can be), there's this: *What about me?*

Those breasts, which have become more like land mines than body parts, more fire than flesh, untouchable. Unthinkable. Too much pain, too little energy. *This is for the baby*, his wife—the new mother—says. Insists. The woman who is still his wife but suddenly much more (and, somehow, a little less).

And what is *he*, now? Something he can't quite identify; something in between husband and father. There's no word for this, is there?

Yes. At last, he understands, there is.

Life. It's life is what it is. What he's thinking about—and describing, and feeling—is life.

(Love? No. It *is* that, of course, but it's something else, too.)

Then, unable to deny, or suppress, or feel badly about feeling it, there's this: If he had known then how he'd feel now, would he still welcome this new life, this part of him, into the world? Their world?

Yes.

(Except when he wants to say *no*. When he feels angry or overwhelmed, and it's entirely his right to have those types of feelings. Because he too has feelings, and he should be able to feel the same way so many other men must feel, at times; tired, emotional, undersexed, even insecure about not being wanted, not being needed. At least that's how it feels, sometimes.)

What about lions? Think about how far we've come. As fathers, anyway. Mothers, throughout nature, and with obvious exceptions, protect and nurture their offspring. It's natural; it's nature. But fathers—mostly—just keep their species going, offering their services as long as required (often, that requirement ceases the minute the baby is born, or even as soon as they've deposited their sperm. Without obligation or reward, they're then on to the next biological adventure). And what of the lions who put nothing ahead of their compulsion to fuck and, when provoked, fight? If there are babies from another father hanging around, they're fair game, they become collateral damage. It's all instinct, part of the whole evolutionary dance.

So, who can blame a human father for the occasional lapse? It's not even a lapse, really; it's an understandable impulse, owed to lack of sleep, maximum stress (itself a signal of compassion, evidence of love), and lack of attention. It's not like you want to *kill* the baby, you just look at her and think: I made you. Or, I too was part of this. None of this is possible without me, you know. So why do I feel scorned? How come I seem so irrelevant?

What about his father? Think about how far he's come. His father wasn't even there the night he was born. Fathers, then, weren't expected at the hospital. After all, they might be at work, or pulling a second shift. Or having a medicinal beer or two at the local pub, no one judging, no one noticing. This is just how it was.

What about his mother? Even she didn't breastfeed. It was a different era, in between old-fashioned lack of options (before there was formula there was what mothers made, nothing in between) and our back-to-the-future paradise of organic everything, where not breast-feeding your baby is only slightly more excusable than matricide. Back then most families made it up as they went along, by necessity, no questions asked. Lack of money meant lack of options, which meant everyone did the best they could and doing your best was good enough.

What about him? When, exactly, did all this guilt become such an unavoidable part of the equation? What do you call that space in between being imperative and replaceable?

A human being. A man. A *father*.

And so, again: he thinks, what if?

If he knew then how he'd feel now…

Yes. Still, yes.

Yes, of course. Yes, a million times. So much yes that a momentary no seems less caustic and almost like a respite, an inevitable, even healthy thunderclap in otherwise cloudless skies.

Yes. But it's okay to say no sometimes. He's only human. His wife, too. And, above all, the baby: part human, part alien, part of both of them. The sum total of everything they said they wanted, and were, in part, put on this earth to do—just like the lions and all the mothers and fathers before them. Something that makes things like paychecks, and townhouses, and retirement, and cars, and careers, and sex fall away like translucent drops of milk from a ragged and aching nipple.

Yes!

Mostly.

LIFE WITHOUT ONIONS

My dude, who hasn't gotten around to proposing marriage but talks about it often, doesn't eat onions. He's one of those people who, if misguided by an apathetic waiter, might taste an unintentional onion in his soup, or in the sauce, or on the not-quite-clean-enough silverware, and turn pale, then begin sweating, and suffocating, and cause a complete scene right in the middle of any restaurant.

This has never actually occurred, yet the possibility exists—and could happen at any time, he insists—so he tends to be obsessive about avoiding allergic reactions. We don't eat out very often. The best way to protect oneself, he claims, is to assume that every meal prepared by anyone else is certain to contain at least a trace of onion, or onion powder, or else has been handled by a fork, or sliced by a knife, that has come in contact with an onion at some point. His diligence makes him a bit abrasive at times, and occasionally, it's awkward to eat with him in public.

But this isn't the biggest problem.

I think he's come to believe that his dread of all-things-onion is a perfectly natural, proper attitude, and not a result of his own anxiety. I'm afraid he assumes my empathy is unwavering to the extent that I myself no longer enjoy onions.

But I do. I love to cook, and you can't cook in a kitchen with no onions. I mean it's not like red meat, or a particular type of food that one can easily avoid. Onions tend to pervade everything on the plate, so it becomes an all-or-nothing scenario. How can you plan a lifetime of meals—pasta, salads, hamburgers, meat loaf, pot roast, chicken kabobs—with the complete absence of onions? You can't. And so, I feel as if I've been unfaithful if I dare to prepare a meal for myself that in any way involves onions. If he even knew that one had been in his kitchen, he'd be beside himself.

Growing up, I had a friend who was allergic to bees; she would tell me about the terrible nightmares she'd have. She wore a special bracelet and carried antidote around with her at all times in case she got stung. Even though the chances of death were remote, she was traumatized by the notion of anaphylactic shock and eventually had little desire to go outdoors. So, I can understand where my dude is coming from, and I know it's not my place to judge another person's phobias as they relate to their health.

But it bothers me, nonetheless.

More than I think it should. Maybe it's simply that I can't imagine life without onions. But that's the way it will have to be if, and when we ever go to the next level. He won't have it any other way, and I'm not the type of person who would keep secrets from her husband, so I can't comfortably exist worrying that I'm cheating on him.

The thing is, he's so intelligent, and intense, it's easy to see why he takes things too seriously sometimes. He seemed surprised when I first mentioned how he constantly talks in his

THIS KIND OF MAN

sleep, and I told him it was because his worry-motor never stopped running. I used to think it was cute, like the way he gets so worked up when one of his teams (he's a big sports fan) loses and he screams and curses at the TV, like they can actually hear him or something.

Maybe it's the premonition I sometimes have, kind of like a recurring dream where I see his compulsion overtaking other areas of our lives. Perhaps, at first, there's a certain type of soap he determines is unacceptable, or that drinking unfiltered water is unhealthy, or that canned soups might cause cancer. Occasionally, I have this terrible vision of living in an all-white house, endlessly scrubbing and cleaning because of all the germs we continuously come in contact with. Or I imagine the way he might act with our children.

Or maybe it's something else entirely.

I've been upset all night, and I'm sitting here in the darkness, watching his fish that always seem to be watching me. I see them swim up and down, from one side to the other, in the same circles, either exhausted or indifferent as the result of being trapped in their miniature world.

He says studies indicate owning an aquarium helps stimulate concentration and creativity. He tells me it relaxes him to look at the tank, how peaceful the fish (who, he reminds me, don't shed, or bark, or bite like other pets) make him feel. I think he'd be disappointed if he knew I didn't share his point of view. The constant activity in that tank inspires anything except calmness, and actually makes me nervous. I can't look at that blur of bright movement without noticing that the big fish is very deliberate, and intent, as it chases the smaller one, over and over, all around the tank, never letting up.

It's probably silly, but it makes me sad, as if I should do something to help. But I know it can't be helped. It's nature's way, and if that little fish wasn't being chased in this aquarium, she'd be getting hunted in another aquarium, or across a lake or ocean somewhere.

I can hear him, chattering away in his sleep, probably solving all the problems from the past day, and anticipating the ones to come tomorrow. I wish I could convey my feelings, to share some of these thoughts with him, but I'm afraid. Afraid of saying the wrong thing. Or upsetting him. Afraid he won't understand me the way I try to understand him. Afraid that if I start talking, I won't be able to stop.

LATER, THAT SAME MORNING

It is still dark.

She sleeps, turning uncomfortably in the sagging, too-large bed. She reaches to feel his body but cannot—he is not there. And then there is light.

She opens her eyes and sits up. She thinks and feels her head, the graying throb, that constant pain. She looks at herself across the room in the full-length mirror. Even from here it's noticeable: a slight swelling, just above her lip. If one were to look closely, the shape of a circle would be discernible. Perhaps, the kind of imprint a plain gold ring might leave. She looks away, quickly, toward the closet, the tight cluster of starched green uniforms lined in still precision like the men who wore them.

The woman in the mirror surprises her. She frowns, realizing what an automatic gesture it's become. And yet, somehow, the more she gazes at herself in the mirror, the less she recognizes the face trapped in the polished glass. Had she grown too accustomed to staring into her own eyes in the hope that, after a while, she might forget? By looking so furtively at what she didn't want to see, perhaps it would further decrease the resemblance of a mother she scarcely knew? Would it ameliorate the misgivings and lost time? Would it explain the secrets? Would it reveal the truth behind the trap doors she locked before opening them?

She looks over at the dresser, the pictures: mostly from the past, only a few recent. Young faces, older faces, the same faces, all smiling in the same strained manner. It occurs to her: *You should only smile when you feel like smiling.*

She absorbs the room, digesting these discordant images that slowly suffocate her as she takes them in. Everything around her is there for a reason, just as there's a reason for everything that surrounds her. The taut symmetry, like a muffled scream: a reflection of her life.

HOW MANY MEN?

It's only been two days and she's already irritated with the sober energy. He gets so worn down and depressed when he's drinking, it's like having an injured animal writhing around in the bedroom. It makes her so anxious, and impatient, she's ready to walk. Then he gets on the wagon and it's as though he's been hypnotized. Up early, doing chores, making plans, wanting to cook, talking about how he's energized; maybe she'd like to go on a run or even a hike with him later? It's exhausting.

Then he gets into a groove. They both do. She can see the pounds come off, the circles under his eyes fade, the glow of life return to his skin. And he's interested in sex. Even better, he can perform. She starts to entertain the sorts of futures she once envisioned. She thinks things like: *this* is what a real relationship is, the inevitable ups and downs, the quarrels and resolutions, all the stuff that makes us grow, makes us real. It then begins to feel too good to last, and she's right, it doesn't. He'll say I feel great, I'm caught up on all my work, God damn it, I deserve a drink. Just a celebratory cocktail, he'll say. And what's the use of working so hard if I can't toast *to* our health and happiness? And then she'll come out at 3 AM and he's passed out on the couch, an emptied bag of potato chips in his lap.

Maybe I'll get a boob job, she'd said. It wasn't serious, though not entirely facetious. It was the type of trial balloon a woman would float to get a guy's attention; the type of thing she'd say to see what he'd do. She knew enough to know that any man, no matter how in love, is never going to be uninterested in a perfect rack. Particularly a perfect rack after 40. That was a statement, not just that the woman was still vain enough about her body to care, but also a statement the man she's with could make to everyone else, especially other men, without saying a word. My woman still *cares*. My woman still cares about *me*. My woman still likes to fuck. My woman still likes to fuck *me*. My woman cares that I want to fuck *her*. The kinds of statements every man will swear are irrelevant, which underscores how relevant they are.

The thing is, she feels guilty.

When they first met, she was so insecure that, at times, it would paralyze all action, even all thought. No, that's not it; the thoughts were never paralyzed. That was the problem. Always thinking, always worrying. Thinking and worrying—about everything. More so than a typical woman, she knew. It was her mother's fault, of course. But her father, with his inability to ever do the right thing; his inability to do *anything*, was also culpable. And she didn't help matters herself. Biology and shitty upbringing aside, she had so many friends, over the years, who had changed for the better. Finding the right partner. Finding themselves in the right classes, or gyms, or on the top of the right mountain they'd climbed, whatever. She'd never given therapy a chance. (Fine, just because it's horseshit doesn't mean it doesn't help a hell of a lot of people.) She had the unbreakable habit of believing men when they lied to her and refusing to

THIS KIND OF MAN

hear them when they told her the truth. She saw all the warning signs and by now it was too late; she was dependent upon her co-dependency. Co-dependency was like the kind of job you're willing to complain about every day but never leave. All the energy in the world to describe, in as much detail for as long as it took, and however often it had to be repeated, but never enough discipline or disgust to make a break. She had acquired a kind of quiet brilliance for not moving on.

So, she was with him. She felt guilty because he had been just good enough. He said all the right things, most of the time. He told her she was beautiful more often than she had any reason to expect. He never once contradicted her when she insisted her parents were as bad as everyone else's, only more so. And he didn't have an instinctive quota regarding the number of times he could say "I love you" in a given day or week or year. He could say it multiple times in a single evening, which she would have sworn was inconceivable—at least in a committed relationship. He had, in short, helped her edge closer to the security she'd spent more than half her life fantasizing about. She wondered if her inclination to leave him was not born of this borrowed bravado. Would it dissipate the second she was alone? Did she not owe it to him to put up with more than she considered acceptable because of what he'd given her?

Then, always at the worst possible time, there was a cameo from one of the three musketeers: anger, silence, or worst of all, tears. Usually in that order. A fight, manufactured or else improvised on the spot, like he's Jackson Pollock, dropping every color on her from the top of a ladder: a red "you're not as sweet as you used to be," a blue "all you fucking do is complain!," a yellow "I used to be different until we got together," a purple "you take everything for granted," a green "I know you think about other men," and so on. At the end, a wet, splattered mess that some rich moron with no taste would interpret as a masterpiece, even though it's the same piece of shit anyone with a paint brush or penis could create. Then the quiet treatment: hours or days (never weeks; even she had limits to how much she'd tolerate); the more she tried to reconcile the more he'd dig in. Then, inevitably, the blubbering. Either because she'd finally give up and ignored him back, or else she'd finally cry herself (she was only human), and the sight of it would make something inside him snap (proving he was human too). And after another session of mediocre make-up sex, she'd ask the same thing every normal woman, in any relationship asks too many times to count (at least she thought): Why can't he stop being such a bastard/bully/baby?

Here's the thing. She *did* think about getting a boob job. She wanted one, too. Except when she didn't; except when she realized it was ridiculous; an ultimate concession to the toxic male shithole men have made the world. But it was, nevertheless, the world she had to make a place in. And if she finally did leave him, how much easier it would be to find another guy with a set of Size C's tilting in the right direction! Also, she *did* think about other men sometimes. She talked to enough friends to understand, even if most of them were lying most of the time, there were men in the world who drank too much and could still get it up. Or who, through vanity, or after enough difficult discussions with their doctors (or themselves in the mirror), cultivated a reasonable balance between booze, diet, and exercise. The all-or-nothing all the time only worked for

THIS KIND OF MAN

rock stars and actors, and most of them necessarily have short shelf lives.

At the end of the day (or, most days) there was this: she'd stayed with lesser men and left better men. You can afford to be picky, or principled, before 40; after that you had to calibrate however you define contentment with how much you fear being alone. For her, now, the idea of growing older alone always outweighed the regrets and resentments, all of which he was kind enough to carry for her in the burgeoning gut above his belt, a volcano fixing to erupt or implode.

Also, this. There's always the chance he'll leave her first. She knows he loves her more, but that's all the more reason he'd do it. A vulnerable man is a desperate man, and a desperate man is an opportunistic man. All a man who suspects he loves more than he's loved needs is a woman he's certain is interested. Not even committed; being interested is enough. A man is just egoistic enough to go looking; just arrogant enough he'll win her over once he has the chance. And if she struggles with how to forgive herself for not getting out while the getting is half-decent, she's not certain she can ever accept losing him to someone else. Someone better. Someone he'll grow into, who will not only understand, but accommodate his foibles, whose weird, inexplicable alchemy will inspire in him previously undiscovered, even unimaginable traits. And her, alone and knowing what all her friends are saying about her, with bemusement or worse, actual sadness: well, look who thought *she* was the only one who deserved better...

And look at him, opening that bottle of white. For all his flaws, how many other men are comfortable and confident drinking white wine? How many men know how to pronounce

Pinot Gris? Even know what it is? How many men appreciate that it's cocktail first, wine or beer after, then a digestif to take the edge off? How many men are willing to cook *and* clean, classical music blaring? How many men read books and refuse to own a TV? How many other men could she pass gas in front of (how many men would acknowledge that women occasionally pass gas)? How many men, either angry or inebriated, at least *attempt* to find a woman's clitoris? How many men would listen to her, when she was drunk, whining about the mother she hates and the father who can't love? How many men are going to understand, on her worst day, that there's a lot lower you can go, because he knows? How many men are going to look at her right now and ask: You're not going to make me drink alone, are you?

INSTINCT

It was, without a doubt, the best night of her life.

She'd known it was coming. The discussions, to her mind, had been frequent enough without becoming bothersome—for either of them—and she'd made her preferences clear while remaining open to the element of surprise (pleasant, of course). It was expected but not *expected*. The primary question was whether he would pop the question on Thanksgiving, or that weekend, or Christmas Eve, or perhaps the next day during their gift exchange. In front of family? Or private?

It being a formality (the good kind), the fact that he managed to surprise her made it that much better.

Casual dinner, he said. Our last night on the town before the craziness and crowds and whatnot. No big thing, he said. Just a night out before we hunker down. Hunker down for the holidays, he said.

It was at the restaurant they'd had their first date, post mutual declaration of love. So...not the *official* restaurant of their first *official* date (which was the one she would have guessed) and, well, she'd figured he was going to wait for Christmas, it being her favorite holiday and all. Nevertheless, a surprise *and* mission accomplished.

Drinks, dinner, dessert, will you marry me. A bottle of champagne and applause from all the other tables. Perfect, the best night ever.

***

She can't stop looking at the ring. She can hardly concentrate on putting one foot in front of the other as they walk to their car. That, and she's a little tipsy.

"Come here," the man says; at first, she thinks he's just another person wanting to see her ring. There had practically been a standing ovation in the restaurant.

He steps toward them: a man about their age. Hat pulled low. Sunglasses at night? Before she can determine if he's a hipster or some drug dealer he shows them his gun. Drunker than she realized, her first thought is: *Seriously? A gun? Who pulls a gun in a parking garage?*

"It's okay," her boyfriend, her *fiancé*, says. "It's okay."

"Give me your wallets," the man says, barely above a whisper.

"It's okay," her fiancé repeats.

"Just shut up and hand me your wallet," the man says, then looks at her. "And that ring."

Drunk, in shock, or both, her initial feeling is one of calm. *No problem*, she thinks. These things happen and so long as no one gets hurt this ring is insured obviously that's what you do when you buy one of these because it's gonna get lost or stolen at some point anyways...

THIS KIND OF MAN

All of this happens before she has time to stop and register what is actually happening.

"Hurry up," the man says, more a hiss than a whisper.

She reaches into her purse and looks at her fiancé. He looks at her and nods. Then he's gone. She screams as he disappears into the darkness of the parking garage.

She looks at the man and sees him looking around, as surprised as she is.

"Shit," he says, suddenly uncertain. Then he takes off running, in the opposite direction.

***

Three things happen as she stands there, alone. First, she begins to shiver as the initial shock—which had warmed her like a blanket of adrenaline—subsides. Then, she realizes how drunk she had been, but no longer was. And last, that her fiancé had left her.

***

"I'm sorry," her fiancé says, again, once they're home. He'd apologized earlier, in the garage, when he pulled up in his car, finding her in the exact spot, phone in hand, not sure if she should call the police, or him, or run back to the restaurant, or hide in the stairwell. He apologized several times during the drive home. Now he apologizes again.

"Please say something," he says.

She doesn't say anything. She isn't sure if she has nothing to say or so many things that it's impossible to speak.

"I'm so sorry," he says, again. "I don't know, I just...I mean, I don't know if it was panic so much as instinct. I think some kind of instinct just kicked in."

She looks at her hand. At the ring, as if it might have some insight to offer.

"You know?" he says.

She looks at him, and then stares at her shoes. The same shoes that had stood in the same spot, alone in that parking garage. After he had run away.

"Please," he starts.

"We need to call the police," she finally says.

***

"I think my feeling was that I could help more by getting *help*," he says, later, in bed. He had said a lot of other things, after they'd given their report to the police. After she had called her parents. After she had emailed her best friends—her future bridesmaids and matron of honor. After he said he didn't want to call anyone, he didn't want to talk about it if she didn't want to. "Do you want to," he'd kept saying. "We don't have to," he insisted.

"I just," he says.

"I thought you didn't want to talk about it." She can tell the coldness in her voice scares him. More than he was already.

"I don't know, I mean, I *do*. I want to talk to *you*..."

"Okay," she says.

THIS KIND OF MAN

"I was thinking, there's always security guards everywhere, all around the shops. It's their fault! Where the hell *were* they when we needed them?"

She doesn't say anything.

"I think, I don't know," he says. "I mean...*I don't know*. Maybe it's best if I stop trying to explain it."

She doesn't say anything.

"I'm not sure I understand it myself. I think it was just instinct, that's all."

Eventually she falls asleep, leaving him in their bed, still fully clothed, trying to find the right thing to say.

***

"Would you rather one of us got shot?"

This is the third time that morning he's asked. Gently the first time, with emotion the second, now with some urgency that sounds just short of annoyance.

"Seriously. Don't you read about how badly these things usually end? We are *so* lucky…"

She doesn't say anything.

"Seriously," he says.

She'd already called into work. She's hungover and slept poorly.

"Do you want me to stay?" he asks.

She doesn't say anything.

"We'll talk more later," he says. "I really shouldn't miss work."

She doesn't say anything.

***

In one of the dreams she'd had that night—the one that woke her up and prevented her from falling back to sleep—they were being held up, again, only this time when the robber (Burglar? Bad guy?) stepped out of the shadows, it was *him*, her fiancé.

***

Her fiancé calls multiple times, and she ignores each one. He begins texting her increasingly frantic messages. R U OK? one reads. CAN U TALK? another one reads. I LOVE U!!!!!, the last one reads. She does not respond.

***

She talks to her mother. She emails back and forth with her best friend. The important thing is you're safe, her friend writes. You should try to sleep, her mother says.

***

Another dream: she's at the altar, at their wedding. As her fiancé accepts the ring from his best man, she turns to the priest and sees he's the bad guy from the parking garage.

"Give me the ring," he says.

***

THIS KIND OF MAN

They haven't had sex in a week, since the night before his proposal, and she hasn't worn the ring since the day after. There are flowers everywhere. Roses from him, a bouquet from her parents, another from his parents, more roses from her best friend, a second bunch of roses from him. She has not been back to work, and her boss tells her to take her time. Work can wait, her boss says. The important thing was that no one got hurt.

***

She's still been unable to sleep, but not for lack of trying. She naps constantly, turning her phone off so the calls and texts (mostly from him) won't disturb her. During her naps she dreams, and they are all variations on a theme. Walking on the beach during their honeymoon and he runs away. Giving birth in the hospital and he runs away. Standing at her mother's coffin at the funeral and he runs away. Laying on her death bed and he runs away.

***

Well, her mother says, then goes on to say a lot of things.

***

Finally, she answers the phone.
"If I could do that entire night over, I would," he says.
"So would I," she says.

***

Three months later she's still not wearing the ring, and everyone has stopped asking her about it.

***

Six months later she receives a letter. Not that you care, but I'm still struggling, it begins. I've been seeing a therapist. He thinks what I did is totally natural. If you can't forgive me, you should at least try to understand. Would it be okay if I'd been shot? Would you still love me, even if I'd been killed?

She stops reading and places the letter in the trash.

***

Nine months later her matron of honor, well, her best friend who was going to be her matron of honor, calls.

"I guess you heard?"

"Heard what?"

"Oh my god, you don't know?"

"Know what?"

Apparently, her no-longer-fiancé is in the hospital. Apparently, there was some type of fight. Something about being drunk, close to last call, a broken pint glass, stitches, mutual charges pressed, a total shit show. So out of character, her friend says. He's like the most peaceful guy ever. The kind of guy who would break *up* a fight, you know?

A lot of questions follow. Yes, I can believe it; I can believe anything. No, you never really know someone, I guess. No, I don't have any intention of visiting him in the hospital. No, I

THIS KIND OF MAN

guess you *don't* have any idea how I actually feel, she says before hanging up, having answered the last unwelcome question.

***

There are other calls, albeit less frequent. I have my own problems, she'll repeat. I have my own life to live, she'll insist. I have had days when I've wanted to die, too, she'll say. We're all going to be dead someday, she says—to herself.

***

A year later she's leaving the bar. A blind date. Decent, she'd see him again, if he asked. She walks to her car, a little drunker than she realized. One drink only on work nights, she reminds herself, smiling.

As she opens her door, someone grabs her from behind.

"Don't move," a man's voice says, barely above a whisper. She recognizes the voice.

"What do you want?" she sighs, wondering why it had taken so long.

"You know what I want," he says.

She turns around and, in spite of herself, is surprised by the face she sees staring back at her.

UNBROKEN THINGS

Question: Who wears a ring on their thumb?

My sister does. And I asked her about it, recently, when she was home for Christmas. She, of course, called it the *winter holiday*; I asked her about that too. This type of politically correct wokeness is everything that's wrong these days: We're too busy trying to fix things that were never broken in the first place with multicultural this, therapy that, and things like thumb rings. What exactly is a *thumb* ring supposed to signify? A statement, no doubt, a code easily identifiable to the Utopian-society, let's-right (or, *left*)-all-the-wrongs-in-the-world-bleeding-heart-professor-types. And to think, we were all so proud of her when she decided she wanted to be a teacher.

Question, I asked: Who wears a ring on their thumb?

Anyone, she said. Anyone who feels like it.

My sister lives in a trailer.

By choice.

From the Ivory Tower to the Painted Desert. She's charted a course that even my experience with her capriciousness could never have prepared me for. A trailer. In the desert. It's too much, the thought of her, hunkered down way out there, without electricity or running water, communing with the coyotes, composing poems by candlelight, subsisting on cactus nectar. For Christ's sake.

Listen: I can tolerate the vegetarianism. At least she's stuck with that, and really seems to believe it does some good, whatever *it* is exactly. If it's not hurting anybody, more power to you, I guess. No matter how idiotic you're being. If the idea of killing something, whether it's a cow or a chicken or a fucking *fish* is inconsistent with the karma you're trying to connect to, that's fine. Who cares?

In fact, I'd be dishonest if I didn't admit I was somewhat envious of those PETA posers. It *does* seem that those who desist from eating meat are invariably healthier than those of us at peace with our opposable thumbs. It's difficult to deny there's something disarmingly sublime about vegetarianism, a nutty nobility these committed individuals are capable of attaining. Something about the self-sacrifice this practice demands that most of us, with our feeble willpower and lack of conviction, are unwilling, or unable to make. Then again, all the hardline vegans tend to be the most self-righteous prigs on the planet, which can be somewhat off-putting.

But my sister is not always in your face about it, or any of the other assorted cultural imperatives she prescribes to. In fact, all of it's so earnest and well-meaning she retains a childlike charm, the type that all those granola girl wannabes she teaches seek to cultivate. In short, she's an innocent, which is why I don't dig the idea of her deciding to run off and disappear in the no-man's land of Ari-fucking-zona.

Look: our family gets together once a year, and I really didn't need to listen to the folks—who aren't getting any younger, and have a hard enough time accepting that their daughter, now in her thirties, is no longer a *baby*—getting bent out of shape and pumping me for details because they know I'm the only one she confides in. They don't even know the half of it. They believed her when she assured them, she wasn't going to be alone, she was bringing her *partner,* some hotshot visiting professor from her department. (*Partner?* See what I mean? See what I'm dealing with here?).

I'll give her this much: it was an impressive, if atypical, bit of forward-thinking on her part. If our mother knew she was actually alone—and there is no way she isn't, because I haven't heard word one about this boyfriend, therefore, he doesn't exist—there'd be no end to the obsessing and handwringing.

Trust me: it was difficult enough showing up without my soon-to-be-ex-wife, and dealing with questions like *if you don't remarry what are the chances of us ever getting any grandchildren?* It would be nice, for once, not to bear the burden of being the golden child, the one with the respectable job (which isn't to say teaching co-eds is not respectable but come on, let's get real here), the one who calls them every Sunday evening even when I'm on business trips, which is often.

It actually seemed, at first, that little sister was going to save the day, arriving with the announcement that the recent publication of her latest book had prompted the adult-diaper wearing deans of her department to grant her tenure. Basking in the double-fisted glow of that good news boded well for me and my plan to divert as much attention as possible from the debacle of my disintegrated marriage. Then the *auteur*, not even

THIS KIND OF MAN

halfway through dinner, drops the bomb, disguised as her bright idea to trek off indefinitely into the Arizona outback. How much she's changed! Such calmness in the crossfire of mother's questions: about her safety, about her sanity, and everything in between. She's learned—I must credit her for that much—she no longer falls apart when the folks put the screws to her.

So: another Christmas, another family feud, par for the course. Being infinitely more sensible than my parents, I assure them that their daughter's enthusiasm will be short-lived. As always, I said she'll savor the shock value, but like the vast majority of her lofty proclamations, little will actually come of it. But then: the frantic call from my mother a few weeks later, saying she got a postcard which simply stated *I'm here* and the number of a P.O. box that she'd try to check every other week or so. Okay, it's for real. For now, anyway. What my mother didn't know *would*, of course, hurt her, or at least distress her. Fortunately, I'm aware of my sister's whereabouts—more or less. All things considered, I save up too much vacation time as it is, and it looks like I won't be spending that week in Nantucket with the wife. So: I figured it was as good a time as any for an impromptu excursion into the dusty void.

Understand: my sister is much more intelligent than her stupid decisions might lead you to believe. Sometimes I have to remind myself of this, since she's always finding new ways to outdo herself. The thing is, when she sets her mind to something, she does it well. Too well. That's the problem: what other people, *most* people, can regard as hobbies, or jobs, or even obligations have always seemed a matter of life and death for her. Once a notion lodges itself in her head, there's nothing half-ass about it, no middle ground: she's down for the count, taking no prisoners, in it to win it, *et cetera*.

Unfortunately for the rest of us, she's rarely encountered a cause she failed to support, whether it was housing a stray dog, or volunteering at some stinking soup kitchen. Name it. A knee-jerker from jump-street, she was prime fodder for the left of center, pro-proletariat haven of university life. Before you know it, she's majoring in English with a minor in Sociology (Sociology!), railing about how the grading scale and standardized tests are hegemonic tools of capitalist oppression, and getting her poetry published in artsy-fartsy literary magazines that nobody but professors and other angst-ridden post-adolescents read. Predictably, she dabbled with drugs, paid lip service (literally) to the free-love farce. If I'd been there, at least I could have slapped some of those pretty boys around, but I was already out *here*, busting my ass and paying my dues. Like I told her, in the real world, the average morning commute will cut any commie-friendly college professor's ideals down to size quicker than you can say *road rage*.

Question: What's the problem?

Nothing, really. Everyone has to go through some shit like this in order to eventually emerge as a sane and productive part of the team. And yet, as always, the single-minded passion that produced those good grades and mostly conforming behavior had her making waves about someday forsaking society and its soulless quest for material satiation. *Et cetera*.

So: a PhD, a book, and a well-earned sabbatical, then *this*. Out to the desert, alone in a trailer with no phone, no contact

THIS KIND OF MAN

at all with the outside world? *Just to be away from distractions*, she insisted, when I coaxed her into telling me what termite mound to look for in the event I needed to get in touch. The only reason she told me was because she knew the last thing I'd ever do is come out and find her. Her enthusiasm unnerved me. What could be worse than all that excess time in the middle of nowhere with a whole lot of nothing going on? Nada. I'd be climbing the walls in three hours. And once again I'm reminding myself that no one knows her as well as I do, that she simply needs someone to look out for her. Which, as a big brother, is what I've always done.

***

During the plane ride I am, as usual, in no mood for casual conversation, especially when I see that the flight is at sardine-can capacity. Now, if your job is one that requires even moderate air travel, then you know my disdain goes much deeper than a simple lack of elbowroom. Which is to say, if you have a low threshold of tolerance for idle chatter with happy-go-lucky head cases or irredeemably bitter creased-collars who, like yourself, can't afford first class (in other words, if you're *normal*), then it's imperative to minimize distractions.

Question: What do you do?

The two sometimes-effective solutions, reading and sleeping are, I've found, ultimately inadequate. Granted, an open paperback conveys the intended message to most would-be confidantes and often will suffice. If, however, you're unfortunate enough to end up beside someone whose personal issues impel them to seek solidarity, your book might be an unwitting icebreaker. Sleeping will work, but who can feign slumber for more than an hour or two? And why should you be held hostage by the perfectly rational disdain for exchanging banal pleasantries at 30,000 feet? The key, then, to rendering oneself *incommunicado* is a simple set of headphones, which leave you at once deaf, dumb, and immune to intrusions of your personal space.

Listen: I used to let things like this bother me, but people are capable of overcoming obstacles. For instance, once I started getting insufferable bouts of bronchitis four and five times a year, it was time to quit smoking. Just like if you can't make the payments on the car you drive, you sell it and buy something you can afford. Spend too much on dry cleaning? Suck it up and iron your own shirts. Then, of course, there are the things you simply decide to deal with. Coffee, in my case, is an Achilles heel. It's my stomach, coffee kills me. Nevertheless, I can't, and won't, go without my morning java, despite my disrespectful stomach. There are just some things you must cope with, and if you don't master them, they master you.

Question: What do I do for a living?

I work, that's what.

And whoever said you were supposed to *like* your job?

My father worked over forty years as a repairman, and I never heard him say a good word about it. He fixed anything: refrigerators, air conditioners, washing machines, name it. He had to spend his days—his entire adult life—going into other people's houses to fix their things. His job was to make broken things work, the things people were too cheap—or too stubborn—to replace, or too damn ignorant to fix themselves.

THIS KIND OF MAN

So, he spent his days inside houses he couldn't afford and would never live in, being reminded of all the things he didn't have. He hated them all, and said it was only the job itself, the process of fixing things, that gave him any satisfaction. Doing the job right, he'd say, is something you can hang your hat on. And so, even as he despised these people whose patronage he depended upon, he went out every day and made their broken things unbroken. He did his job.

I understand how he felt.

The thing is, I'm worried about my sister. There's always been something about her that was too much like a tragedy waiting to happen. So far, she's had a remarkable run, going pretty much unscathed, but all of us have our day, sooner or later. If she wants to write her poems, teach coddled yuppies-in-training how to decipher that poetry, drink green tea, practice yoga, and even wear a *thumb* ring, that's fine. But going out to the desert? Alone?

Question: *Are you happy?*

This is what she's always asking me. What is happiness, I say. This would turn the tables on just about anyone else, but not her. I usually get some sort of lyrical gibberish by way of response. Do you know what she wrote when she inscribed my copy of her latest book? *People are like snowflakes: they are more alike than not, but despite the similarity of their splendor, no two are exactly the same.*

Where the hell am I supposed to go with that? You see what I'm dealing with here?

I'm happy, she says.

What is happiness, I say.

***

Question: What happens if she's not there?

She isn't expecting company, and as I drive the rental car away from the airport it occurs to me, for the first time: what if she's not there? Unlikely. Where the hell else is she going to be? Besides, if I told her I was coming, she might have made it a point *not* to be there. So, I'm content: the element of surprise can only work to my advantage. Not unlike the Conquistadors, who had a surprise or two for the Indians when they arrived, uninvited, with their Spanish flags and swords. Then, later, the missionaries, who found that the sword was not nearly as mighty, or successful, as the tongue—especially a tongue that spoke so assuredly of the heavens or hells awaiting us all, depending upon our faiths in the Spanish-speaking God. The Mormons swept through this place, as did the displaced Confederate Veterans, and the opportunistic would-be entrepreneurs who rushed after the deceptive siren song of the gold mines.

There was not much any of them were able to do to tame or subdue this dry ocean of gray earth. And perhaps that's precisely what entices the itinerant souls who are drawn into or driven by this serene, sun-blanched soil—an expansiveness that seems to solicit order and adaptation. I imagine this sense of possibility is what appealed most to my sister, and her poetic sensibilities. To be sure, there's something almost inexplicably inviting about the crimson sun setting slowly over this space, the acres upon acres of open, still uncharted *space*. The air is

THIS KIND OF MAN

extraordinary, clear and dry, the type of air your body wants to breathe, and you can sense the appreciable contrast to the stifling smog of the city.

But it quickly passes. Because while the differences are drastic: no cars and congestion, or crowds of commuters, there's also the *lack* of these same things which, for me at least, provide a sense of security. The rhythm of autonomy is not altogether unappealing. The routine, plodding as it can be, still serves a purpose: it reminds you you're alive, a functioning part of a system; a bigger, better cycle. To remove oneself from the mechanized march, to step outside of time, couldn't actually lead to some sort of authentic enlightenment, could it? Not for my money.

The earth begins to open up, as though the air is pressing the ground low and wide. It's been about an hour, and I notice the occasional trailer. This means I'm getting closer, but I'm already thinking about how far I've come, and how long it will take me to get back. Something's begun to bother me, the way you'll wake up in the middle of the night with a scratch in the back of your throat and know in the morning you're going to be sick.

Finally, I see a trailer that more or less resembles the one she described to me. There's a car out front—not hers—and I pause, uncertain whether I should stop or keep going. Before I can decide, the door swings open and a woman walks out. She's slightly older, and heavier, and less familiar, which is always the case. But I still don't recognize her. Then my sister walks out and stands beside her.

Question: Who is surprising whom here?

Okay, I think. One of her professor friends is visiting. No big deal.

My sister gives me a hug and introduces her friend.

"This is Noel, my partner…"

Comment: Not Noelle, *Noel.*

Question: *Partner?*

She's about forty, I figure, but looks at least five years younger: perfectly coifed ponytail, necklace with the new-age turquoise crystal, and of course, two-dozen or so stud earrings. There's more metal than cartilage in those ugly, abused ears. The only thing preventing her from being a walking mid-life crisis is that she's very obviously a professor—she's *always* been this way. Sandals, canvas smock, the obligatory stench of patchouli, she is appropriately absurd. I hate her already.

"So, *you're* the brother I've heard so much about," she begins (I'm not saying her voice is deeper than mine, but if I saw that voice in a dark alley, I wouldn't not be concerned), holding out her unmanicured man's hand.

I ignore her and turn to my sister.

"Partner?"

She gives me a look.

"I mean when you say *partner*, you mean like the two of you are writing a book together or something, right?"

She gives me a look.

I turn to her partner.

"So, *you're* the boyfriend I've heard so little about…"

THIS KIND OF MAN

He gives me a look.

"Listen, there's no need to be rude," he retorts.

Apparently, he's used to being addressed more respectfully by his colleagues and students. Which is fine with me, as I didn't come all the way out here looking to make any new friends.

My sister asks me to sit down and offers me something to drink (sorry I don't have any beer or anything like that, she says), and the initial tension is, unfortunately, eased. Suffice it to say, significant wind has been stolen from my sails. I'd anticipated a more intimate encounter and am being forced to adjust my strategy on the fly. Fortunately, I do that for a living. But as we sit around and idly shoot the shit, I can't help sensing *I'm* the only one who seems ill at ease. I have to give the kid credit, she's utterly unflappable, as though she half-expected me to show up.

I have the privilege of hearing all about the *partner* she didn't deem necessary to tell me about until now, and he's happy to elaborate on all the adventures they have planned. Noel, who asserts he is part Cherokee Indian, is doing research for a book on indigenous cultures; my sister is accompanying him on his excursions. Whatever the hell that's all about. Needless to say, I see through this charade like thinly sliced Swiss cheese. He *does* have a vaguely ethnic look, I guess, which he probably disliked intensely throughout his childhood, until he found himself in academia—where it could be used to his advantage. Now, clearly, he's content to milk it for every ounce it's worth, as though to make up for lost time.

He sure can talk.

My sister and I barely get a word in edgewise while he elaborates on the reasons he's always preferred sleeping outdoors, under the stars, to the comforts of modern life.

"So, tell me," I interject, holding up my hand. "Have you ever actually done an honest day's work?"

"I spent a summer loading crates, if that's what you mean," he says, with precisely the piqued tone I'd hoped to provoke. "And if it wasn't for my scholarship, I would have had to put myself through school."

"I bet you would have," I say.

My sister, who has been staring at him, full of wonder and approval, gives me a look, again. I don't bother to acknowledge his reply, but wave my arm dismissively, as though he's a fly buzzing outside the screened porch of our conversation.

"So, are you getting any *writing* done?" I ask her.

"Yes, it's very peaceful out here, and naturally conducive to creativity. I think this will be a very productive time for Noel and me."

Question: What's going on?

It occurs to me that the room is very warm (how the hell can you live out in the *desert* without electricity?) and I realize the two of them have continued talking (for seconds? minutes?) but I haven't heard a word they've said. For all I know they've been making jokes at my expense, right in front of my face. And just like that, it's on: I was not, as usual, able to feel it coming, but suddenly the air is suddenly, sickeningly thin. Then, that sluggish feeling of being suffocated, a heart attack in slow motion.

THIS KIND OF MAN

Question: What's going on!

The first time I remember this happening, I was waiting for another routine flight to take off. As we waited our interminable turn on the runway, I became convinced the oxygen had somehow been released from the plane; for several seconds I couldn't breathe and almost made a scene. Almost. Since then, the incidents have not been infrequent. Sometimes it's in a traffic jam, or in a cab, or worst of all, in the middle of the day, for no discernible reason, simply while I'm sitting at my desk, attempting to be productive. It reminds me of when my sister and I used to swim in the lake and try to touch the bottom. It was always the same, going down in warm, brown water that got colder and darker the deeper you went, and the pressure eventually made your ears pop and your eyes bulge. And the awful part, struggling to get back to the top for air, those few moments where you could *see* the surface glistening above you, but not getting there fast enough. That panic, that fear of dying. This is not something, as a grown man, you feel comfortable sharing with anyone.

What's going on?

They're both looking at me, and I'm not sure how to interpret the look on their faces, but I don't like it.

"Why are you sweating...are you okay?"

It's him, he is right in front of me—too close—and it is definitely not concern, I decide, but amusement on that smug, smiling face. There's no doubt he is laughing at me.

Question: What would *you* do?

Before I can decide, I've already taken a swing and missed. He doesn't miss. And the next thing I know I'm looking up at both of them. Him with his fists still cocked, and her with a dumbfounded expression that probably mirrors mine. *Laid out by a lesbo*, I think, *by a woman!* That just figures, my hippie turns out to be a ringer.

"Are you okay?" My sister.

I don't know yet. I can't feel anything, and keep repeating to myself: laid out by *one punch*...

Despite my humiliation, there's a rather large burden lifted—at least now my sister can put *him* in his place, show him where her loyalty lies.

"I think you should go." My sister. (Again).

I'm so contented with the satisfaction of my expectations that I don't understand why *he* isn't saying anything. Only then do I look up and realize she's talking to *me*.

Then I feel it, finally. The pain, like a wasp's sting under my eye, the letdown of this violent energy that's been slowly imploding, back from the moment my wife told me she was in love with another man, the exhaustion from the plane ride and solitary drive through the nowhere land of this god damned desert, the bitter sum total of my own defeats, all of it. Everything.

Question: What am I doing?

All of the sudden someone is sobbing and that someone is me. Sobbing! I haven't cried since I was a teenager, but the waterworks are going now and it's too late to stop them.

"Noel, can you please leave us alone for a moment?"

"Sure, of course, I'm sorry..."

THIS KIND OF MAN

He holds out his hand to help me up and that's too much. Shrinking before both of them, I turn my head away, practically hearing all the school kids gathered around the sidelines, scoffing at the class bully who just got bitch slapped.

Nothing happens for a while, but I can *feel* her staring at me, that face, the concern, her shame. That face, which always wanted my help, or used to anyway.

"Are you okay?"

"I'll get over it," I say, still unable to look at her.

"What's wrong?"

"Nothing, it's not like I've never been hit before..."

"No, I mean what's *wrong*? Why did you come all the way out here?"

Finally, I look over, and her face looks exactly like I knew it would. I wonder what *my* face looks like right about now.

"I just...I figured something was up...and I needed to know *what*..."

"You know, you're just like our father."

Okay. So?

"Well, what if I am? What's so wrong about that?"

"Nothing, I guess. It's just...you don't understand, I'm *not* like him, I never wanted to be..."

"So that's why you came out *here*?"

"No, I came out here because I wanted to, that's all. Now tell me, why are *you* here?"

I came out here, I guess, because I needed to.

Question: Why?

"I don't know. I guess the folks and I were worried for nothing."

"Worried? Why would you be worried about *me*?"

"Are you saying we shouldn't be?"

She rolls her eyes and shakes her head.

"I mean what do you expect," I say. "Do *normal* people just run off and live in the desert?"

"*Normal* people live their lives, and allow others to do the same…"

Ouch.

"What are you trying to say?"

"I just wish that all of you would let me live my life!"

Well, that changes everything. Her cry for help was really just a polite request to be left alone.

Question: What happened?

It doesn't make sense, or even seem possible, seeing the tables turned so decisively. So suddenly. This is the same girl who, while never causing any real trouble, always seemed to be *troubled*, complaining about how our father never showed her enough attention or support, so ardent to express her alternative points of view. For so long, she was the black sheep, and everything followed accordingly. A family cultivates certain expectations, and if someone stops playing along, it throws a big wrench in the machinery. When had she decided she no longer needed, or wanted, our approval? Perhaps she never did, or she just got over it. Over us. One thing seems certain: by getting away, she's attained what we wouldn't have encouraged her to

THIS KIND OF MAN

seek and has become all the things we never envisioned her being. And it kind of kills me.

Question: So why is *she* crying?

"You're my big brother, and I'm looking at you, telling me that you're concerned about me…and I feel like I don't know you. Or that you don't know me for that matter."

Nothing like a little salt for the open sore. She might as well be telling me I don't know myself.

***

I'm out of there. What else can I do?

Sometimes things need fixing, even if they don't seem broken. And sometimes you just need to drive away. So, I'm driving. Past the sand, and those trailers, and all the strangers I'll never meet. People who may have come out here to get away from something, or to embrace something they couldn't find anywhere else.

Not for me. It's too hot, too clean. Too *real*. Give me the city any day, and as many different cities as possible. Enough so that, after a while, all the places look the same, and the faces all blend into one another. Everyone knowing what's expected of them and going about it, living their lives.

Question: What's wrong?

It's okay, you can tell me, she says, sounding much more like a mother—or a wife for that matter—than a kid sister. *What's wrong? Why are you so unhappy?*

Nothing's changed, even out here: it's the same old story. *I'm not*, I insist, smiling even though it makes the shiner under my eye sting like a son of a bitch. *I'm not unhappy*, I say, feeling like a priest who has celebrated mass millions of times and suddenly, one day, discovers that it's just so many fancy words. *I'm not unhappy*, I repeat, over and over, even as I drive away, as though by saying it enough times, I might make one of us believe it.

As I get closer to the airport, I'm already improving. I've forgotten most of what happened, and my eye is mostly numb. Numb, my whole mind is numb. Kind of like a bad dream, it seems so vivid and disorienting when it scares you out of a deep slumber, but then you wake up and quickly get busy, losing yourself in the routine. (Again). Or, if you're lucky, you're able to drift back to sleep.

OUR VIETNAM

First off, I apologize.

The phone is going to ring. It's going to be me. I need you to answer it.

I'm sorry. I know you don't want to take this call, because you're an accessory. But you're an accessory, so you have to take this call.

Remember, after you showed up last week and said you were taking me to get help; that it was time to check me in somewhere, I asked you (okay, I begged) to give me one more week, to see if I could get clean on my own, once and for all? And the email I sent yesterday saying it had been three days and I hadn't had a drop? I was lying.

Here's the deal: if you're going to save my life, you need to roll up your sleeves and get involved. I can't promise it will be painless, but that's what friends are for, right? Don't worry, I'll game plan this all out for you.

This is our Vietnam.

That's the last card in the deck and I have to pull it. Which one of us first came up with that line, anyway? Who am I kidding, you came up with it, of course. You always came up with all the good ones.

Don't pretend like I don't remember your own little breakdown. Sophomore year? We didn't call it *anxiety* then. *My brain broke,* is what you said. What was that like, really? Because I have a feeling I'll need to get used to that kind of thing going forward. Breaking my will, breaking my balls. Everything broken. Really though, was that just something you got therapy for? Did the meds really kick in and set things straight? Did you change your diet, or what? Don't tell me it really *does* help to meditate and listen to music, like you've always said. Please tell me that's not how it works, because I don't think that's in the forecast for me. I just don't see it, and we both know I do love music. To be honest, I'll need something more than that.

Remember the time I took you to the emergency room? That was junior year, when we moved off campus into that crappy apartment. Four guys, one bathroom. Still the best place I've ever lived, all things considered. Anyway, remember when we were out on the lake and you had your shirt off and got burned? Your whole back was red, like we boiled you in salt water. So you kept putting aloe on it? And you woke up in the middle of the night and thought your skin was falling off? You said it was like when your foot falls asleep only it was everywhere from your ears to your asshole? It turns out you put on so much aloe you dried out the skin. Who knew? Turns out it was too much of a good thing. You thought you were helping but you basically drew all the moisture out of a sunburn, an allergic type of reaction. So you stood in the shower, because only the water hitting it would stop that itch, like a million bug bites. You actually thought you were going insane, remember? I kept telling you this was your Vietnam and you finally screamed at me, told me to stop. Thing is, I wasn't even joking. Not totally,

THIS KIND OF MAN

anyway. I mean, if you could have seen yourself you would have understood. I knew you were in pain, but I've never seen you *scared* like that before. Like you did something permanent, like you seriously messed yourself up. We had to go to the ER and they gave you some steroid cream, worked like a charm. That really was your Vietnam, wasn't it? One day tour of duty, bailed out by over-the-counter meds. What a tough guy.

Well imagine how you felt, but this time the part where you stood in the shower wasn't working. Just standing there, no relief, nothing but crawling out of your own skin. That's how I feel right now, except on the inside. I've felt this way for weeks. I mean we always joked that every bad hangover was another Vietnam; this is a whole different level. It's enough to make you contemplate doing something drastic. Like…

What I'm saying is, I'm scared.

How about you? Afraid of the hard truths? Don't be. There's nothing you'll say that I haven't been through in my mind at least a thousand times. Usually at 4:30 every morning, an existential alarm clock, my conscience (or at least my consciousness) dehydrated and desperate for something I can't give it. Not anymore.

How long have I known? Longer than you'd think, longer than you'd believe. Way before Missy left me. Before I lost custody of Conrad. Before I even lost visiting rights.

I know everyone thinks the bottom fell out the night I went to jail. If I'm honest, that wasn't even a lowlight. How many of us dream of slugging our father-in law but never have the opportunity? If you're going to get arrested, you may as well *earn* that shit. Do you know how much I fantasized about it?

You think *you* know what a sanctimonious prick he is? Remember when he read the entire wedding party the riot act for drinking before the rehearsal dinner? How uptight he was on what should have been one of the happiest days of his life? You don't know the half of it. Believe me, he had it coming; it was practically a love tap, what I gave him. I should have left him dead on the living room floor is what I should have done. When that son of a bitch tried to press full charges, he confirmed everything I ever thought about him. And then some. Man of God, right? You should have seen Missy trying to convince him he was making everything worse, like she was a lawyer. She did talk him off the ledge, but neither of them ever let me forget it, that's for sure. Anyway, if I never have to see that asshole again, there's at least one silver lining in all of this.

I swear to Christ I think he's actually gay. Seriously. And no, that's not a cheap shot. Missy would tell me every now and then that her mom would complain he never touched her. And you've met her mom, Nancy. She never says anything, and it's not like she gets a loose tongue when she drinks. They never drink! I mean, they're the kind of religious nuts who don't even have wine at church service. You remember the wedding.

I'll tell you something I never admitted to anybody, not even Missy. I went to her old man, like I should have, you know to ask him for her hand and all that? That bastard said no! He refused to give me his blessing. That was another time Missy and her mom had to convince him he was making a mistake. Now, he can tell them he was right. That fucker.

I may have grown to hate myself (believe it or not I can remember a time when I didn't), but I never really hated the

THIS KIND OF MAN

alcohol. There's a reason I never did drugs, I never wanted to. But I always enjoyed drinking. Except when I didn't. Even on the worst days, all that guilt and all the promises, I still felt like I was getting more out of it than it got from me. I don't blame the booze though, that's the pussy way out. Plenty of people can handle it without fucking up their lives. You, for example. You've always been able to take it or leave it. At least you seem like you balanced it out, just like you eat soup the night after you have steak or drink sparkling water the days after you get hammered. I know you quit jogging, but you're still walking, right? Walking! To think we both played soccer back in the day. You never got married but you manage to still get laid. You seem to tolerate your job or at least it tolerates you. I'm not saying you're *happy*, because nobody is. At least not in America. And if people can't be happy here, we're all truly fucked, a bunch of babies who want everything they can't have. All I wanted was another drink.

Look man, you're going to need to try harder than you did last week. We'll need to go deeper. Deeper than we've ever gone. Deeper than guys usually go. Definitely deeper than I ever went with Missy. I'm going to have to talk about *everything*.

I'm sure everybody thinks she stopped sleeping with me. Well, she did, but the marriage was done way before then. The truth? It was worse when we were still having sex. Way worse. You've never been married but you probably can at least imagine someone going along with it because you want them to, because they feel like they have to. I'll let you in on a dirty secret: a woman can be crueler by sleeping with you than refusing you. Have you ever been on top of a woman who not only pretended she was dead, but let you know she wished she *was* dead? It makes you despise her, and yourself, in ways you've never imagined. But you still go through with it because you *have* to (that's the difference between men and women; they can turn it off in ways we can't fathom, ways we shouldn't ever *want* to).

Remember how you used to get all the girls? Maybe that ruined you for commitment, and that's why you're still a bachelor. Are you really trying to tell me you're happy? I usually couldn't get the ones I wanted, but Missy was the one I held out for. Of course, you remember, you helped me close the deal, for Christ's sake. I went all in, put every chip on the table. Confession: I even prayed; I mean I think I literally sold my soul to have a shot with her. And look at me now. What I'm saying is, I'd take her back if she'd have me. Yeah, you can say I blew it, that I ran out of chances, that it's my fault, not hers. But what about sickness and health and all that crap? She bailed when the going got tough. Fuck her!

And fuck you, too.

Hey man, sorry about that, but there's going to be some outbursts. I can guarantee that. And don't get all high and mighty either, we both know you've got a temper of your own, so imagine how I feel. I'm not even saying I won't take a swing at you. I don't want to, but let's face it, if your life has become a cliché, what else can you do but dive into the deep end? No use dicking around in the kiddie pool. If I'm drowning, I'm not going to drown in two inches of water. Plus, you could always take a punch. What are friends for, right?

I don't want to go through this alone. I don't think I can. This is where I need you to be honest, like one thousand

THIS KIND OF MAN

percent. Be a real friend and level with me. I'm not worried that by giving up or surrendering or whatever fucking mantra I'll have to repeat ten thousand times that I'll feel like a loser. I know what I am. I've known this was coming, unless I died in my sleep, for a long time. What I'm worried about is what everyone else is going to say. I feel like I've kept most of our friends in the dark. Do they know? Have I been kidding myself? Does everyone already talk about me that way? Between us, I hope not, because then that's something *else* to feel shitty about. I held out this long because I can't stand the idea of losing everything and still having people pity me.

What do I come back to, after this?

And don't make me any dumb promises, okay? Like we're going to hang out? Please. You know I'll have no choice but to hate you. We both know it's inevitable (not personal, strictly business, ha ha). I'm not going to see any of you guys again. As good as you've been to me, and especially if you step it up now and come through when I need you most? I'm going to need to lean on that and use all that gratitude as anger. It's the only way I see through this, without resorting to religion, and fuck that shit. But who knows? Maybe after they get done with me, I'll come out wearing a cross, going to church, listening to gospel music, the whole goddamn shebang.

You know what I'm saying, right? Even after all this I don't have it in me to kill myself.

Remember after 9/11, we said "this is our Vietnam?" That was true, but it was also a bunch of bullshit. I mean, aside from making airport travel impossible, what did any of us actually give? Those poor suckers sent to Iraq and Afghanistan? *That* was *their* Vietnam. What I've realized is that life is our Vietnam. Just being born; the war begins and we all know, right away, how it's going to end. Man, I hate hospitals. How did you handle that, when your dad was dying? I guess you just do what you have to do.

Let's talk about you a little more.

I know you've never gotten over losing your father, and we both remember he could be a real hard-ass, how you guys had the whole love/hate thing. I never told you this, but do you know how much I wished I could have had a relationship with my old man? Do you know what I'd give to have one memory of him and me connecting in any adult way? I'm not blaming him for all my problems, but becoming a father really clears up what kind of effort your own parents made. Whatever, we can't blame people for being who they are right?

Me, for example.

It's not that I can't imagine life without booze, it's that I can't imagine *life*. How do people fill all those hours? Do I really want to go to the gym every night? Worrying about my abs or watching calories in my 40s? That's even more depressing than puking in the parking garage before work. I'd rather sneak out to my car before lunch for some warm hair of the dog than tracking my fucking steps each day. You probably count your steps, don't you?

Fine. Tell me more about your philosophy, how it's all about balance. I mean, you put on the extra ten after college, but you never let it get to twenty. Is that the secret? Or is it simply having one less beer each night? Did you really swear off fast food when you turned 30? How is that possible? The road to hell may be paved with potato chips, but at least it tastes good. I mean what's the point? Are we really supposed to spend our lives trying to cheat fate when everyone dies no matter what? I'm not saying we have to balloon up like your mom did after what happened with your dad (no offense, and you know I love her). I mean she's always seemed happy, right? What, don't tell me even *she's* unsatisfied? I don't know if I can handle that. She's learned to live without your dad, I guess we just have to learn to live without things we used to have.

Even when we were kids, she seemed happy to be there. Your pops, too. At the swim meets and shit? I know my parents were there because they had to be. They more or less came out and told me so. I know how much I hate my boy's baseball games. Do you know how awful they are? They never end! I realize you think your folks were hard on you. Do you know how lucky you were? I know it seemed like my parents spoiled me, but it's easier to just buy kids stuff instead of, like, talking to them. Believe me.

I've never been one to talk. I suppose that's all about to change. I promise I'll try not to turn into one of those happy-go-lucky born-again types who always sound like they're trying to sell you something. I'm not making any guarantees, but if I have to lose my dignity, I can at least delay it as long as possible. What can I say? I mean, what else am I supposed to tell you? I'm laying it all out on the table. It doesn't even hurt as much as I thought it would, but that could just be the whiskey talking. We'll see what happens when you take it away. From my cold, dead hands (ha-ha).

Anyways.

So, like I said, your phone is going to ring. It may be in a few minutes, maybe a few hours, even days. It may be never, hey, I may still pull through. But I wouldn't be telling you all this if I wasn't ready for a change, ready for...something. And you're the last one, the only one I want to talk to. Or the only one I want to listen to. Let's pretend we're in school again. Maybe I'll get my Springsteen albums out. A little *Darkness on the Edge of Town*, for old time's sake? "Prove it all night," right? Maybe one last beer? Or my first sparkling water, whatever.

But the phone is going to ring. And you'll be ready, at last. Finally, you'll be prepared. You have to be. There's only one thing I ask, just one thing I expect. There's only one thing I hope you'll say when you pick up that call, after all these years. You know what I'm talking about, right?

Please tell me you know what I need you to say.

IV

STILL THIRSTY

What are you waiting for?

He did it again, was thinking it, again. The first time he caught himself asking this question, he felt so guilty he could have horse-whipped himself. Five, six ER visits later, he didn't feel anything. Eight, nine? He actually cared, he really wanted to know. How long will it take?

His son's refusal to die is killing him.

A one-man show with plenty of drama, but little flair; a slow-motion suicide with neither ardor nor élan. No swan dives from the top of a parking garage. No Russian Roulette with a full clip. No drowning in the bathtub or walking into the ocean with pockets full of rocks. The thing is, he doesn't want to die—he still wants to live. To drink. He remains, somehow, after all of this, still thirsty.

And it's *his* fault, naturally.

(The sins of the father…)

It runs in the family, and that, he knows, is the kind of inheritance one can always count on. He's seen it, ripping through his family tree like, well, a razorblade through a wet wrist. An instinctual taste for it, or else the inability to have a taste and just leave it. That's the gateway, they say. Actually, it's the gasoline you swallow to douse some fire, ablaze deep inside, and all it does is conflagrate. That fire gets going, reaches all the way to the heavens and back down to the hell where it originated, and this panacea turned poison—including everything from cheap beer to the best liquor, from a stealthy shot in the closet to a desperate digestif in the middle of the night, from bottle service at an inane night club to a swig of mouthwash—is all you crave, never too much, always the cure for an unquenchable thirst.

His wife has taken a bathroom break, leaving him alone, leaving him susceptible to the thoughts and questions he is mostly able to avoid, as long as he's not alone—with his thoughts, with the inevitable questions.

Question: *What are we waiting for?*

The doctor. Doctors, he's learned, are not unlike priests, particularly if you're dealing with a chronic and seemingly uncontrollable disease. You look to them for guidance, you hope they'll offer absolution. And in either scenario, chapel or hospital, it works best for those with faith. When you're young, faith is another word for hope; you believe because you want something; you have faith because you need it. When you're older—and have both received and been denied things that can be explained by pretty much anything but your faith or lack thereof—you find yourself alone, and with a lot of questions.

Question: *What's taking so long?*

He's still thinking about the doctor. Mostly.

THIS KIND OF MAN

This isn't his first rodeo. If you'd caught up with him at pretty much any point in the last ten to fifteen years, he'd have a different story to tell. And he had all the time in the world to talk about it. About his son. About himself. There wasn't enough lukewarm coffee in the world to accompany his testimony. He could have spoken, at length, about the hospitals, the doctors you at first revere and then come to despise, how the nurses are the ones doing all the heavy lifting and are not afraid to get their fingers dirty, how the system provides just enough resources and common sense to ensure the exact same things keep happening. The salmon shoot downstream, trying to break on through to the other side. Most die trying. Whether it's because of a bear, or gravity, or lack of character, not all fish are created equal. Or else Nature needs to experiment with socialism. Something.

He could have talked about group therapy, the 12 Steps, the hollow eyes of the hopeless and the barren eyes of the hopeful; the frightening eyes of the converted. The deadened eyes of a father who has searched abandoned buildings, smelling smoke and shit and walking through literal broken glass while looking for his son. Thinking things like: I changed his diapers and saw his baby private parts and thought suitable fatherly thoughts. Such as: one day he too will be a father, and the cycle will go on.

A whole different cycle has set in, and he long ago discarded dreams about being a grandfather. That salmon set sail, got snatched midair, and digested by an indifferent grizzly. And there it is, right now, his fantasy of the future a fetid pile of bear shit, all over his shoes and almost slippery enough for him to fall inside of, forever…

Hey, I'm you, he thinks. He'd gotten lost inside himself, again. He's become an expert at this routine, equal parts necessity and self-fulfilling prophecy.

Okay. I'm here. What am I doing?

This is what he'll look like, he thinks.

No, that's a different thought. A new one. Did he actually just envision what his son would look like, dead? Yes, but he's done that before; how could he not, after what they've endured? No, he just envisioned that he *was* dead, with the accompanying thought: what's taking so long? For him to be at peace? For us to stop ruining ourselves with worry and fear and anger? For us to move on, whatever that entailed?

Guilt unlike any he's ever felt, or even imagined, soaks him like an impossibly dry sweat as he looks down at his son, eyes shut and off in never-never land (or perhaps maybe-maybe land, where there's still some possibility of getting to wherever he's always trying—and failing—to arrive). He's breathing, slow and calm, the equipment and high-power meds doing most of the work, all this apparatus going above and beyond, enabling these fallible specimens to survive, all these frail patients with unique personalities and life stories that couldn't be more dissimilar except for the fact that they were identical.

Our son's in good hands, he's thought about ten million times before, standing in the same spot, looking at the same sight, thinking the same thoughts.

Hate the sin, not the sinner.

Like the church says.

THIS KIND OF MAN

I don't hate you, I hate your addiction.

Like they teach you to say, in therapy.

I don't hate myself.

Like he's been saying, more often and with less conviction.

This is the part of the story where the hero catches his breath, no longer able to recognize these thoughts and the person thinking them. But he can't, and won't, because he has no problem whatsoever reconciling these thoughts, the person having them, or what, exactly, took so long for him to admit these things to himself.

Water, he needs water.

To take an endless swig and keep drinking until he pisses out all these thoughts and questions and mostly the regret in his gut.

Having a hangover never helps. Having a hangover in a hospital is even worse. Having a hangover in a hospital, because your son is laid out after another overdose, is getting to unduly complicated levels of self-loathing.

But last night he'd given up, for a few hours. For a few hours, he focused entirely on himself and what he wanted. What he needed.

He got drunk. His wife got angry.

It's been the consistent and predictable pattern, at least lately and with increasing frequency: One thing follows the other: he drinks; he gets drunk; his wife gets angry.

His wife, never a big drinker, had, somewhere along the way, cut out alcohol entirely. That made things occasionally uncomfortable for him, but she was an adult, and he was an adult, and so on. But after the fourth or fifth *crisis* she suggested he stop drinking. After the sixth or seventh it was more like a demand. And whether it was stupid male pride, or the fact that he needed to determine for himself the things he could control and take responsibility for, or that, at the end of the day, he didn't especially want to stop drinking, and at the end of the night, he really needed that drink, it became a growing wedge between them.

It had escalated to the point where he'd wait for his wife to use the can or take a shower so he could grab a quick belt—always pulling out the ice cubes like a lab technician handling fissionable materials, trying to avoid the telltale clink. She'd always know, whether from seeing that same highball he'd forget to put in the dishwasher five minutes or five hours later, or because his mood noticeably changed after the first few sips, or just the ways wives know everything every husband does, particularly the things he tries to hide. Another door opened when he just stopped pretending, and now she simply frowns every time he opens the freezer.

His wife is back.

Eventually, a husband realizes, the only thing worse than never being able to read your wife, is always being able to read her. Always knowing when she's disappointed, which becomes easier when she seems to be disappointed all the time.

(More guilt: His son's crisis had been the best thing for his sex life. At first, anyway. Nothing quite like an ordeal to pull a family together—or the opposite, so when you acknowledge it's the former, and not the latter, it's emboldening, contagious, a turn on. There was the stress-relieving sex, the *we're-in-this-together* sex, the *you're-the-only-thing-I-can-rely-on* sex, and the good old-fashioned fucking, the kind most couples forget about and either can't recall or don't need after marriage and certainly not after kids. But the resolve, or peace, or whatever it was, that resulted from this unexpected and welcome closeness was like the sex itself: necessarily short-lived and increasingly difficult to recreate.

Eventually, they recognized theirs was a scenario that neither love nor money, or experts and out-patient institutions could adequately address. It was going to be a combination of tenacity, luck, and faith if there was any chance whatsoever. And worse, no matter what they did, and no matter how tenacious, lucky, and filled with faith they were, it was, ultimately and entirely, up to their son to determine whether things would ever improve.)

"What did I miss?" she asks, and he is genuinely unsure if she's being serious.

"Are you serious?" he asks.

"Okay, so I'm assuming the doctor didn't drop by?"

No, he says, to himself. Not in the five minutes you were away.

He shakes his head.

"My turn for the bathroom," he says.

This is the part of the story where he ducks out to find the chapel, to gather his thoughts. To prostrate himself and ask, again, for mercy. For help. For anything other than what's presently on offer. But he knows he won't do that; he can't do it.

It's another door he's already passed through. In order for any intervention that's not of this earth to occur, you must have faith. You have to keep the faith (what else can you do? Just accept that there's nothing?). The problem is that's a revolving door that only goes in one direction. The good news: you are free, not reliant on the absurdity of cults and fantasies—you are, in short, no longer a child. The bad news: you're completely on your own.

Father, please hear my confession...

Bullshit.

He'd actually gotten up and walked out. What the fuck did he have to confess about? For being a straight-A student and getting a scholarship? For being a good husband who never strayed, or felt particularly tempted to do so? For ascending the corporate ladder, but not stabbing any colleagues in the back, or screwing over any subordinates to get where he was always headed? For paying all his taxes, and coaching little league, and mostly staying off the sauce on weeknights, and never blacking out on weekends except on special (e.g., awful) occasions? For doing homework with his son and watching every god-awful Disney movie ever made? For being That Dad during slumber parties, making popcorn and cleaning up the spilled soda and not getting angry when the boys made too much noise after bedtime? For wishing with every fiber of his being that his son would turn out okay? For actively praying that he could take the proverbial bullet if it meant sparing his son the fate he

THIS KIND OF MAN

seemed to be irretrievably securing? For not once blaming God, for never one time even bringing Him into it, and not because of fear but because of a genuine sort of humility that's the essence of fealty—the acceptance that we're flawed vessels, etc., and that we had all the tools at our disposal, etc., and our free will is our biggest blessing unless we blow it, etc., and God can't be expected to create everything, manage everything, and look after each life because what are parents for, etc.

Eventually, inevitably, he'd quit the church.

Only because it quit me first, he'd think anytime that Catholic guilt raised its self-righteous head.

He used to envy the hard cases, the stories of martyrs, especially Holocaust victims who, even as they suffered the worst at the hand of their brothers (had anything really changed from Cain and Abel?), still declared their mercy and forgiveness? Now he hated them. What weaklings, what cowards. What kind of character do you have if you're being starved to death for no reason and you still die with love in your heart?

A drink.

What he needs now is a strong drink. Of course, they don't serve booze in hospitals, and for entirely good reasons. Except for, where else on earth are people in more desperate and justifiable need of a stiff cocktail?

When a situation like his becomes unmanageable, you either give up or you get professional. He didn't have a flask because he'd put away childish things, and even though that was the groomsman's gift at every wedding he attended in his '20s, he had no use for them. Only men not old enough to use flasks buy them, and anyone old enough to use one is too embarrassed to do so. So, he'd actually bought one; the one he carries now, the one out in his car.

He steps out into the hallway, past the white coats scurrying here and there, somehow frowning and smiling at the same time, as only doctors can do, and finds the elevator. On the way down to the lobby it stops, and an older man gets in (a grandfather, he decides). They exchange a quick, cordial nod. It's a gesture that stops short of being formal, or friendly, but it's considerably different than the look strangers customarily give one another in a public place. The difference, to anyone else, would be all but imperceptible: this exchange of empathy, this implicit solidarity. It's a communication given and received exclusively in hospitals, where no one entering or exiting is free from the peculiar burden compelling their visit.

Good luck with whatever you're headed toward, they say to each other, silently.

Outside, at last. He can feel the sun, that unblinking life force. He looks up, cautiously: You learn not to stare into the sun—it's dangerous and even worse, it's a cliché. What is the sun going to tell you, even if cared to acknowledge us, even if it *could*? It's enough that it's there. He's grateful, at least, for the clarity of its glow, the fact that it does its dirty work during the day, making it possible (impossibly) to light up the other stars, operating under cover of darkness. These stars don't say anything, and they don't need to; *at least we can see them*, he thinks. They are there, no matter where they came from, just like we're here, no matter where we're going. They were there before we got here, and they'll be there long after we're gone. Humbling, maybe even horrifying, but there is nothing we—or they—can do about it. It might not be enough, but somehow it has to be.

If all else fails, enough people come to understand—and possibly take comfort in the fact that—you can always talk to yourself. *You* know who you are and you will always hear your voice, even when you don't want to. Even (or especially) when you're not sure what you can tell yourself; when you're not at all certain what you can, or should, or may say.

"Here's the thing about our ape cousins," he'd said, the night before, dropping the cherry into his Old-Fashioned. "They don't have performance reviews. They don't worry when they go gray. No mid-life crises to be concerned about!"

He took a big sip.

"They don't covet their neighbor's wife. Or what the hell do I know? Maybe they do!"

His wife glared.

"But you know what, they also can't enjoy a single barrel bourbon!"

His wife, having used up her limited supply of bemusement, patience, and anger, allowed him to continue along like this for as long as she could tolerate it, and when he finally stopped talking (so he could focus on pouring another drink), she looked at him meaningfully and asked the same question they'd each had asked each other, themselves, and potential higher powers, so many times before.

"What's going to happen?"

In his mind, he'd already auditioned several possible replies.

Everything will be better this time.

No.

Everything will be worse.

No.

Everything will be the same.

No.

I have no idea.

No.

I'm beginning not to care.

No.

Is it okay if I don't care for a few hours?

No.

I need another drink.

Okay.

"I'm going to have another drink," he said.

His wife glared.

"I mean I'm just focused on things I can control," he began, but she was already walking away. Which was okay: There was another Old-Fashioned that required his attention.

This is the part of the story where, if he could, he'd erase so many similar conversations, so much of what he's said, especially lately. Like magic, like in the bad old days when you typed up your reports and had to use white-out to revise certain

THIS KIND OF MAN

words, or lines, or omit entire passages—nothing digital and no way to easily improve or change. But life is impossible to erase: you can't unsay things you've said, undo things you've done, unthink things you've thought.

Big Macs for breakfast, he thinks, remembering another conversation he'd replace with harmless, or at least non-incriminating white noise, if he could.

"If this situation has convinced me of one thing," he began, and the way his wife tensed up made him wish he wasn't going where he'd already committed to going. (Too late, if you think it, it's already a sin!)

"I'm going to eat more red meat. Drink more red wine. I'm never eating kale again, and fuck Brussels sprouts!"

His wife looked at him a way she never had. With sadness.

"Because you want to get cancer," she said.

"What's the difference? We spend our whole lives running in fear. That lightning is either going to strike you or it isn't."

"Not if you stay inside," his wife said.

"But who wants to stay inside all the time? That's my whole point."

They notice, simultaneously, that his highball is empty.

"All I'm saying is, it's going to get ugly for all of us, are we really not supposed to enjoy the ride?"

"Only someone who's never seen cancer can say things like that."

"Only someone who has never gotten over her mother dying of cancer would think that," he said, and immediately regretted it. But screw it, he was in knee-deep a minute ago; now he was soaked. Time to start swimming, or drowning.

"Only someone who has spent nights in the hospital, watching a horrible illness take over someone's entire system, yes," she said as he refilled his glass, forgetting—or not needing—the fruit this time.

"Only someone who has tried to explain that yes, you need to be intubated again, and yes, once again they couldn't remove the tumor, and yes, you're only allowed to have ice chips even though you're so thirsty you would drink toilet water," she said.

"All I'm saying is that what's the difference? You suffer then, sure. But we suffer now. Is it really worse, being doped up and feeling no pain, knowing exactly what you're up against, instead of worrying and not enjoying the here-and-now because you're so terrified of what *might* happen?"

"Only someone who's never seen cancer can say things like that," she said, getting up and leaving the room. Which was just as well, as he was ready for round four.

At the car, finally, and he feels like he's back in high school, sneaking a drink from his dad's liquor cabinet. The old take out some and refill it with water routine. Here he is, a grown ass man, looking around guiltily as he grabs a quick pull from the flask. The fire water, lighting him up, like a fried battery getting some juice; a stalled car receiving a few drops of gas. But still, the guilt; something else our ape cousins don't experience—only humans (made in God's image!) feel this intolerable guilt, even or especially when they shouldn't, because, after all, we're only human.

THIS KIND OF MAN

(More guilt: He was through with therapy.

Admission: therapy didn't hurt. It may not have helped, but it didn't hurt. He was mature enough, he was *man* enough, to concede that, mostly without equivocation.

He learned some interesting strategies. He learned, for instance, to breathe. Seriously, it's so underrated. Especially when you're having a panic attack. And it's possibly the only thing that works after you've drank yourself to sleep (as usual) and woken up in the middle of the night (as always), agitated, confused, and gasping for breath, certain you're about to die, or at least have a cardiac event. Unwilling to wake up your wife because you're embarrassed. Afraid to wake up your wife because you've already done that too many times. Unable to wake up your wife because she's sleeping in another room.

Once you've gotten your breathing under control you begin thinking with breath. One thought follows the next, a flow state broken down to its most primordial element. Like animals, unencumbered in the wild, never forgetting to breathe in and breathe out. They also never forget that something is constantly trying to kill and eat them; in that they are most unlike humans. Or most alike, depending on one's level of cynicism.

So, one breath repeated, one thought following the next. If my son stops drinking, I can focus on myself. If I can focus on myself, my wife can worry less. If my wife worries less, I might have normal marital relations. If I have normal marital relations, I might not always need to drink myself to sleep. And so on.

If there's one thing he would change, aside from his son's illness of course, it would be the pity. That's the worst part of this, the way everyone in his life now looks at him like a prototype instead of a person. In everyone's world, there's the person who lost a parent, the person who got divorced (or, these days, the person who stayed married), the person with the perfect kid, the person with the kid on the spectrum, the person with the kid who might play pro ball, and the person with the fucked-up kid. They worry for him, they pray for him, they thank every benevolent force in the universe their own kid isn't like his, they wish they didn't have to deal with him, they pitied him, and his wife, and their son, and all the other parents and children in the world who were also fucked-up and, increasingly, beyond any hope of getting the help or lucky break they so desperately needed.)

Everyone, these days, knows about the stages of grief. Less understood are the stages of denial, but he could write a book about them. Denial is a coping mechanism, sure, but it's also a function of evolution. He can trace his own journey through the various hospital stays, the *crises*. These crises, he has come to understand, are the events preceded by the practice runs and the post-game analysis. In some weird ways these crises present the rare moments of calm, because they seem to be the only times when no one is in motion, dreading what's about to happen or already happened; they are perversely precious occasions when everyone is present (trapped, even) in the here and now. Human beings, like all animals, are accustomed to their routines and rituals; without them confusion and danger seem inevitable. Unlike other animals, human beings, with their big brains, have memories and the types of relationships obliging them to remember things they'd prefer to forget.

THIS KIND OF MAN

Hence, denial. Thus, the book he could write. The history of his stations of the cross, acted out over years in different hospitals.

First time: an accident; could happen to anyone. Second: bad luck; every child needs a few bad breaks to break even, and for every setback there's a stroke of good fortune. Third time: hey, this is actually a *good* thing; at least now we know it's an issue, something to keep an eye on. Fourth time: okay, we can't kid ourselves anymore, this is a problem, and thank Christ we are smart enough and have the resources to do something meaningful, something that will stick. Fifth time: this is going to make him stronger in the end, it'll make us *all* stronger. Sixth time: it's not his fault; this is genetics, and really, is anything anyone's fault? Little kids get leukemia, do we blame them? Of course not. This is the same thing, and worse in a way; at least the innocent kids in the critical ward get unbridled support and sympathy. Seventh time: if any of these doctors and counselors knew what they were doing, we might have made some progress. I mean what are we paying for? Eighth time: I was too hard on him; I bought into all that bullshit about activities, and sports, and making him get a job. Why couldn't I just let him be a teenager? What was the hurry? Did he need to understand accountability and responsibility? Couldn't I have kept giving him allowance and let him be a boy a bit longer? Despite everything I promised not to do, I'm just like my old man. Ninth time: if I'm honest, this is his mother's fault. She's always been too lenient; lets him get away with everything. No boundaries, no lines in the sand. Do people obey the rules because they know it's the right thing to do? Of course not, they act right to get rewarded, or avoid being punished.

Ninth time was not the charm. There was never any charm, and the situation became increasingly less charming as they fumbled their way through one false start and crash ending after another. That was when his lack of faith turned into a different type of faith—a faith that there might not be a bottom and that the worst would just keep coming, the way it always does. It was when he first asked the question no father (no friend, no *stranger*) should ever ask; the first time he asked, in a voice he could, at last, neither deny nor suppress: *What's taking so long?* And it was, finally, when a different sort of door opened. The moment he turned on his wife (even if it was a momentary lapse, the result of nerves, and lack of sleep, and the sort of frustration that only a father in his situation could possibly fathom), there was a certain something—solidarity, naivete—that he could never, from that moment going forward, retrieve. And worse, he didn't know, until after, that he was (also, finally) catching up to where his wife had already been, years before. Blaming him.

It could be worse, he thinks, watching the man (Older man? *Old* man?) slowly pull the old wheelchair out of the old trunk of his old car. Presumably about to go pick up his old wife from inside this old hospital where she's hard at work dying of old age or some disease old enough to have been cured by now—except for death, which no one can ever cure.

(On that score, he'd been lucky: no hospitals, no bedside vigils for his parents. His old man at his desk at work, a stroke taking him out instantly, like, well, like an act of God; his mother in her sleep at the nursing home. Their deaths had not prepared him for the slow-motion disintegration of his son.

THIS KIND OF MAN

He'd always secretly appreciated his luck (and the obvious karma of his parents, being good people, and their quick, painless deaths). But maybe it was something else, and a different kind of karma had awaited him.)

He feels pity for this man, who will slowly wheel his wife from the reception area or the waiting room or her bed, or wherever she was, waiting, all the time in the world to think about how little time she had left in this world. But she knows her husband is coming for her, and he'll slowly bring her down to the car, slowly help her in, and they'll slowly drive home where they slowly go back to the routine they keep in between trips to the hospital. And so on. Not that long ago this entire scene would have depressed him, but now it fills him with something like envy.

He thinks about his own wife.

When they brought the kitten home from the shelter, shortly after they were married, the first thing his wife did was ask him a question he couldn't answer.

"What are we going to do when it dies?"

At first, he wasn't sure what she meant, or if she was joking.

"I mean, I don't know how I'm going to handle it, being without her," she explained. Then he understood: she was already imagining the loss, far in their futures, of this brand-new life, and the void it would present.

"I don't know," he'd said, and he meant it on many levels. As in: I don't know how we'll handle it, because I haven't given it any thought. And: I've never had, or lost, a pet before, so how can I imagine what it might be like? And mostly: I have no idea how to console, much less comprehend this kind of empathy, the intensity of this commitment (the commitment of this intensity?). It was this lack of guile and excess of compassion that he cherished about his wife. If she can become this attached, this quickly, to an animal, this is a woman I can stay with, he thought. A woman I can have a family with; a woman I can grow old with.

There was so much he didn't understand, then.

There was so much he didn't understand, now.

But a few things he knew, definitively: kittens don't drink, or have babies who grow up and do drugs; kittens don't have hangovers or forget to return calls during business trips; kittens don't have sexual needs, or need their laundry done, or their dishes washed, or their checkbooks balanced. Mostly, kittens don't say the wrong things at the worst times. Unlike husbands, or the sons they're named after, kittens are, more or less, predictable from the day you rescue them to the day you put them down.

(More guilt. Once more with the sins of the father and all that. Having a kid who is killing you might make you consider the Old Testament in a new light. All the filicide that seems, to an altar boy, so appalling. Who knows what was really going on before Our Father who Art in Heaven flooded the land? Maybe the people he created in His image forced him to pull the plug, throwing out all those babies in bath water made up of the Holy Trinity's tears. Not a massacre as much as a reset on humanity, to be repeated as often as necessary. Maybe Abraham was fed up with his prodigal son, sipping too much blood of Christ

THIS KIND OF MAN

(although Communion hadn't been invented yet), or The Big Guy Himself, standing by while His son had nails hammered into his flesh for sins never recorded for the final record. It doesn't mean any of that eye-for-an-eye stuff is more palatable, but it tends to confirm that the oldest stories simply recycle themselves.)

The thing is, they really have checked all the boxes. Rehab, full support, tough love, distance and forced separation, capitulation and enabling, unwavering support, disillusionment, embarrassment, semi-complete clean slates all around, threats made, promises broken, threats kept, reconciliation, regret for bonds that can't be severed, guilt for bonds that were severed, back to square one, unbearable futures faced, resignation, and finally, something close to but worse than apathy.

When you're a parent nothing is a metaphor or microcosm, it's just the same scenario unfolding in different ways: you always see your baby, the life you brought into this world, in need of protection, worthy of unconditional love, no questions asked.

But still, there are certain circumstances when your child really does become a baby again. Those moments, becoming conscious in a hospital bed, all fear and innocence—before the defense mechanisms kick in; before the song and dance of ritual humiliation, repentance, and so many promises starting fresh; there are those moments where you see the unencumbered potential and the promise you made to him (and yourself) when you became a father.

Eventually, he found himself entertaining thoughts that made him question his education, his political views, and his religious beliefs. Like: everything we think we know about animals is wrong. Animals have an instinctual ability to identify and root out the weak ones; to a human watching the mother hen pecking at the one slightly deformed baby or the puppies shutting out the runt, it's appalling, and the desire to intervene, to help, is overwhelming. And understandable. But humans are wired differently, due to big brains, evolution, and that whole in God's image thing.

My only job is to have him outlive me.

That was his first thought when he laid eyes on the new life that had resided inside his wife for nine months, this miraculous extension of them, pulled from the safe uncertainty of her womb into a world with a to-do list already in progress; he was already late for all the things that would be expected of him.

Life is a gift *and* life is a curse. Is that it? Is that the best he can do after all he's been through?

(More guilt. Yes, he'd added it up. The days spent worrying? The fights with his wife? No, he couldn't count that high. But he *could* review his bank statements. The rehabs, the therapy, the medication, the everything above and beyond what even the most optimistic or generous father could ever plan— or prepare—for.

And worse, he'd counted what he could have bought with that dough. Three new cars. Sixteen trips to Hawaii. Season tickets to every game of his team (any team, any sport) for life. Enough investment to provide safe drinking water for entire villages in other countries. And so on. Or, he could have built a bonfire in his front yard, invited all his neighbors over, and thrown hundred-dollar bill after hundred-dollar bill into the flames. How futile and childish would that have been? Very. But it would have given him much more pleasure than watching his son dry heaving, or dropping him off and picking him up at any of the various, equally horrific treatment centers, or driving past the church he no longer attended because fuck any God that would do this, or any of the other billion things He decides to do, as though people that pray to and fear Him are a bunch of useless worms, or looking at the fresh stitches on his son's wrist, or his own face in the mirror at pretty much anytime during the last decade.)

He reaches for his flask, and it feels light. He picks it up and puts it to his mouth. Empty.

(Less guilt? He'd been the teetotaler, sort of. He mostly abstained, and it was for all the right and respectable reasons: he had a job to advance at, he had a reputation—inside and outside the office—to uphold, they had a kid to raise, etc.

And one of the running jokes was: all the things he'd do once he could lighten up, let go of the societal and familial pressures. *An actual three martini lunch...or just a martini for lunch. Or a martini for dinner!* Or: *No more jogging and no more diet-anything.* Or: *No fat? How about more fat!* And his personal favorite: *Big Macs for breakfast.*

What would he change, knowing what he knows now?

That's the question he's mostly been able to avoid answering, but he finds himself asking it more often, and with increasing impatience.)

His phone rings.

He feels it vibrate in his front pocket, an abrupt reminder that the real world, with all its urgencies, awaited him.

Who was it? Could be his wife; could be his sister. Could be work; could be a telemarketer. It could be God, a miracle on the line, ready with the water turned to wine, about to teach him to be a fisher of men, whatever that meant. And here he was, flask in hand, ignoring what, for all he knew, was divine intervention. Story of his life: Sorry Fate, I was on the other line.

He knows what's next.

From the ER to that *other* place. Another door you go through, equal parts confession and badge of honor. The Emergency Room is, after a while, a cakewalk, at least compared to the Psych Ward. At least in the ER they're actively trying to save you; their job is to help. At the Psych Ward, they're just keeping you alive long enough to let you go. And they won't let you go until they're good and ready, and they're never good or ready. It's like purgatory, except you're not waiting to get into heaven so much as hoping to get a fragile reprieve from something worse than hell. We imagine hell as a place of ceaseless pain and suffering, but at least when you're in distress you know you're alive; the only thing worse than feeling terrible is not feeling anything. We might, from a certain perspective,

THIS KIND OF MAN

envy a human being with no ability to think deeply enough to understand pity or fear or aspiration; for the highly medicated patient—healthy in all ways except for the ways their unhealthy habits have impaired their functions—it must be like being an insect trapped in an upside-down jar while sluggish giants slowly inspect you.

In the Psych Ward, his son mostly sits on his cot and stares at the wall. Which was, he supposed, the point. At least for people in his state. Ashamed and angry, he refuses to say anything, like he's having a quiet tantrum from toddler years— a game of wills to see which parent would break first (one of them always did, he now remembers with decidedly mixed feelings). But the silent treatment was not the worst; he'd saved that for the most recent visit, when he just laughed, as if to acknowledge the pitiful predictability of this cycle.

Question: What behavior, no matter the cost or consequence, will we tolerate?

Answer: At this point, pretty much anything.

Being in the Psych Ward, he used to hope, was like being in the Drunk tank: it's where people have epiphanies that begin and end with the fact that they never, under any circumstances, want to find themselves in such a place, ever again. But his son, he's realized, has been in bleaker places. And he's gone through his own gruesome door and found those places are endurable. Because, no matter what he does or where he goes, he's always stuck in the one place he can't abide and will never escape: his own skin.

(More guilt. He has, on more than one occasion, wished they'd tried for a second child. No one ever considers a sibling a fallback plan (do they?), but everyone plays the percentages, at least if they're smart. And he was smart; or at least, he was educated, a man who understood evolution and the myriad factors involved in any animal making it from conception to birth. But it had been his decision to hold off, wait until his career was more established, their financials more settled, their permanent house acquired, etc. And what happened? Time does what it does, elapsing like a fast-forwarded video, featuring blurred images of birthdays, holidays, vacations, promotions, and the thousand trivial contingencies that occupy decades like so much rain inside a cloud, all of which is about to get dumped and then dried up.)

He's not even my son, he thinks.

That was another one of their jokes.

Anytime his son left food out or spilled something without cleaning it. "Your son made a mess," he'd say to his wife, and they'd laugh.

Every bad report card or the minor infractions cured by groundings or withheld allowances. "Your son is at it again," he'd say.

The thing is, he'd carried it on; either an inside joke with himself or a defense mechanism. "Your son is in the holding tank," he'd said the first or second time, before even this most inside of jokes was no longer an opportunity for humor.

Another car totaled. And so on.

It went from being a quip to a kind of mantra.

THIS KIND OF MAN

This *couldn't* be my son, he'd think, each time. No way this is *my* son.

His wife settled into a sort of psychological battle mode where she no longer lingered on the past or obsessed about possible futures; she was focused on the present moment, processing everything and dealing with it, like a job—each setback another task to be completed, a long list of checked items. It was her ability to accept, even embrace, the ugliness that initially made it so difficult for her. Over time, he's come to understand, it's how she's found the peace and purpose to deal with it in ways healthier, more positive, and admirable than he could comprehend.

This is the part of the story where he hopes his wife, worried, wondering where he'd gone off to, comes looking and finds him. And in that moment, it's clear: she cares, she's still concerned about things other than if, and when their son will return to them (return to our world). She's worried about their not-so-happily ever after, worried about *him*—the man who'd put that ring on her finger and a house over their heads, the man who had done everything he could, including conceding the things he couldn't, because that's what makes each of us human, because that's what men, who carry so many unspoken burdens, need to know: that the woman they love will love them until death do they part. Or, the death of a son.

It's a nice image, but one he can't maintain, even as abstraction. His wife has long since given up, on him, if not their son, and it's time for him to embrace the clichés of failure: see the writing on the wall, play the hand he's been dealt, and do whatever it is a man does when there's nothing but closed doors and silence surrounding him.

(More guilt. Does he wish his son had never been born?

Been there, done that. That's old news and, if not resolved, acknowledged. No, it's at a whole other level now, a level he would never have imagined possible, even when they were more than half-way into this never-ending mess. He finds himself now, and not infrequently, wondering if it would all be for the best if *he'd* never been born. And that gets to an uglier place in a hurry. Once you begin not caring if you didn't exist, it's not a long way to the next exit where you don't especially mind if *nobody* existed.)

Here's the part of the story where he gets back in the car and takes off, taking it upon himself to finally make some decisions.

Like driving home right now, pouring out four fingers, or however many it will take to keep the Scotch sluicing around his tongue until, mercifully, he can't think or feel anything at all.

One final door to walk through.

Out to his garage, where he'll wait in the running car as the exhaust works its invisible magic, like incense in an old church—this holy ghost the one that will actually show up, addressing, at last, all his unanswered prayers. At last, a certain way to shrink this spiraling world and its too many problems to count down to a size in which he could finally sleep, but forever.

THIS KIND OF MAN

Maybe, after all this, the last question is one he asks himself.

What are you waiting for?

WAITING

He waits.

He looks out the window and he waits.

He doesn't look at the magazine, the one on top of the others littering the table, the one last picked up by the last person who sat in this room.

He stands, not wanting to sit, not wanting to look down at the magazine. He looks down at the magazine, which stares up at him, defiant, disinterested. The magazine didn't ask to be brought into this room, it didn't ask to be read or ignored, to be picked up and put down, to be digested and then discarded.

He stands, knowing that if he thinks about the magazine he wishes he wasn't looking at—the magazine he won't read— he won't think of the things he doesn't want to think about.

He doesn't walk into the corridor to look into the room that his wife isn't in.

He waits.

He understands—anyone who has been where he is understands—that you must prepare yourself to wait a long time. So, you prepare, and you wait. And then, it's even longer than that, longer than you remember. Much longer. He remembers: standing, then sitting in this room, almost the exact same spot, twice already (*third time is the charm*, he doesn't think) and still can't help being surprised at how long he's had to wait.

He waits.

No one talks to him (they know who he is and why he's here), and no one knows the story he could tell (it's the same story everyone who has stood where he's standing would tell).

He stands silently, shifting and sorting his awareness that, eventually, they'll bring her to the room. When they bring her to the room, he'll see her. He'll see her seeing him, then see her seeing him see her. And then she'll ask him, and he'll have to tell her. He'll try not to tell her, and she'll look at him and remind him that he has to tell her.

He waits.

He wishes they would hurry up (*hurry up and get it over with*, he doesn't say) and then he hopes that they'll never come so he can stand, peacefully paralyzed.

Eventually, he looks at the table, and the magazine that waits for him to pick it up. He doesn't pick it up.

He sits down and doesn't think about the nothingness that surrounds him, the nothingness around him, and the gnawing nothingness inside him. He doesn't notice the plants, or the paintings, or the cheerfully colored curtain that doesn't quite cover the light outside. He doesn't allow himself to contemplate the sterile silence screaming all around him, the vacant spaces, and the odd energies of dying life. Most of all, he doesn't think about *it*: how impossibly clean people, in impossibly white clothes, speaking impossible to understand languages, using impossibly powerful tools and technology do everything they can, but still can't keep *it* from occurring.

He finds himself staring, again, at the magazine; the magazine he's picked up without realizing it. He doesn't open the magazine that, under normal circumstances, he wouldn't have the slightest inclination to read. He doesn't open it and therefore does not, among other things, learn about which foods would improve his sex drive and help him sleep more soundly, he does not find out ways to make his partner reach new levels of ecstasy *every time*, he does not peruse his horoscope to see what the future has in store for him, he does not discover the secret to losing ten pounds in only three days, and he does not skim the interview explaining how the fragile millionaire singer lost the chance at making millions more dollars after having a nervous breakdown while filming a commercial for a soft drink she wouldn't otherwise endorse.

He waits.

He doesn't pass the time planning opportunities that could create happiness. He doesn't deceive himself (this time) about the possibility of forgetting the present by focusing on the past. He doesn't dwell on the types of things they would enjoy doing again; the things they enjoyed, once, which they never found the time for, or always forgot to do. He doesn't think about the ways you discover the things you love, *then*, become the things that bring about inexplicable sorrow: the movies, the music, the meals, the books, the board games, the photo albums, the family.

THIS KIND OF MAN

And so: he doesn't allow himself to think about her as she is now, or how she was then. Or how he is now, or how he was then. How he will be.

He looks down at the magazine, again, and picks it up, again.

He understands that the second he opens the magazine they will arrive, wheeling her down the hall like the enigmatic magicians they're trained to be. If he opens the magazine, the magic act, performed (again) before an awkward audience, will begin. So, he waits.

He stands up and looks out the window, at the horizon, beginning to disappear in heavy air beneath the tops of the trees. He looks down, far below, where miniature people inside miniature cars sit in miniature rows, slowly moving forward in the direction of their miniature houses and the miniature respites awaiting them. The sky continues to sag, ensnaring the world in its unspeaking sentry. The people, and then the cars, and then the earth all slip away, leaving only lights that sigh stoically, bearing witness to it all. He looks down at the waning waves of lights, and these lights do not look like a thousand sets of eyes, they do not make the darkness more discernible, they do not appear as poetry. They're exactly what they are: they are progress, they are pain, they are power. They are the cold crucible of machines that control the lives of the men who make them.

He doesn't let himself think about these things. He has too many other things not to think about.

He doesn't turn around.

He'll hear them, eventually, when they come.

Eventually they will come, and he will hear them, and then he will turn around.

Then, he will...

He looks down, again, at the magazine he will not read. He knows, again, that if he opens the magazine, they will come.

He sits silently and stares at the magazine. He stands and looks out the window. He does not turn around.

He waits.

GETHSEMANE

The first thing he realizes is that he's awake and thinking about his father.
Or is he still asleep, and dreaming?
He opens his eyes and looks at the faces looking at him.
He's been here before. Not just literally, either. He has envisioned it, more times than he'd care to count. The near-deathbed experience, surrounded not by friends, or family, but impassive professionals.
Okay, I'm ready, he thinks. *Let's get on with it.*

He knows why he's here. Aside from the fact that he's dying. He's *here* because he's still alive. He's still alive because he hadn't had the nerve to do what he always figured he'd do. What he promised himself he'd do. What he promised himself he'd do, if the time came when he was facing what he'd seen his mother endure. What his mother endured, exacerbated by the fact that she'd watched *her* mother endure the same, only worse. A curious inheritance handed down successive generations: the fear of some certainty, neither premonition nor resignation, just an inability to forget, and a refusal to deny what was, eventually...inevitable. Even if cancer wasn't the culprit, some other sort of death was, and no one who dies before they're ready (is anyone ever ready?) can be said to have died *happily*.

Nevertheless, he had, finally, been unwilling to do himself in as he imagined (hoped?) he would (could?). There were at least two reasons for this, aside from cowardice.

The first, his grandchildren. His daughter was going to have to deal with enough once he went, anyway: the coffin, the funeral, the insurance, the paperwork—all the mess he'd dealt with after his parents died. It was unbearable to imagine how his grandchildren might react, especially as he was convinced his daughter would tell them the truth. They would be mortified, or worse, frightened (angry?). No matter what damage he'd done, or the negligible good he'd counteracted it with, imparting trauma to the only two human beings he loved without reservation, was not a possibility he could tolerate. So, no ugly—if expedited—self-imposed ending.

The second reason was surprisingly simple: he wanted to live.

You can't just turn it off. Or else, you must be badly wired, or past the point of reason. Or very, very brave. And committed. Plus, as bad as things had become, they weren't...*that* bad. The physical pain he could, for the most part, handle; anticipation, he knew, was half the battle. He saw what his mother had faced, and knew how much easier, relatively speaking, it was today. His mother, and especially *her* mother—those were times when the treatments weren't as advanced and the medicine was not as effective. Add to that the ridiculous implications of religious belief; that any type of assisted death was an affront to God's will. At least his father had been out of the picture by that point,

THIS KIND OF MAN

having seemingly made his own deal, or else had his prayers answered: heart attack, one and done, here and gone. It was arduous enough helping his mother over the finish line without Mr. "The Lord has a plan" insisting faith was more effective than morphine.

He had figured out that existence was an unending stream of pain and boredom, occasionally punctuated—if we're lucky—with good times, which become the memories we cling to like life rafts. And a little perspective never hurts. Imagine being in Calcutta, or Somalia, or just about anywhere in the world, without means, without a chance. If Catholicism had equipped him with one advantage, it was an ability to appreciate how comparatively lucky he'd been; how anyone born white and not a woman had zero excuses from the word go. It prepared one, however morbidly, to confront the disappointments and despair.

About the despair: The discomfort, the inconvenience, the relentless dissipation of vitality, all these things he had foreseen. But nothing, he'd found, and come to fear, could adequately prime you for the *mental* aspect. Everyone knows at some point we simply…go to sleep. We don't feel anything anymore and are released from consciousness, certainly from our suffering. But all of that occurs once biology (chemistry?) takes over. Getting from here to there? That had proven more difficult than he'd anticipated.

So here he was, waiting for something he couldn't control, a conclusion he couldn't orchestrate.

The spirit is willing, but the flesh is weak.

Searching (still?) for some way out, not yet ready to let go, anything (still!) to avoid the inexorable.

Father, if you are willing, remove this cup from me.

So, *this* is what it was like: alone, finally, time to walk forward into…nothing. Even the son of God had his moment of doubt, abandoned in the garden of Gethsemane. And if He could waver, what hope was there for anyone else? What, after all, was *He* afraid of? He was *God.* What was crucifixion, a few moments of agony compared with an eternity of bliss? Peace everlasting, et cetera. The MVP of all of us, for all time, honored forevermore. Who wouldn't volunteer for *that* assignment?

Hey, are you up there? Is anyone listening? Make some noise, for Christ's sake!

Do you have your affairs in order?

Doc, that's how I got into this mess in the first place, he'd wanted to say. *That's a good line*, he'd thought. Damn shame he'd never have the opportunity to share it with anyone. It was too flippant, too unserious. Too true.

The joke's on me, he'd thought, the day he received his diagnosis—the one he always knew was coming for him, like an intractable collection agency.

How long? he didn't ask. It didn't matter. From everything he'd heard, and seen, it was always quicker. Always. Besides, he'd already made the obligatory effort, the whole *Let's try chemo and beat this son of a bitch!* Had it helped? Perhaps it had bought some time; most likely it had prolonged things, all those days paid for in puke, incontinence, insomnia, and the inability to feel like a human being for even five seconds on any particular day.

But he'd dealt with it, because that's what one does.

Maybe if he'd had someone to talk to, someone he trusted, they could have spit-balled the options, calculated risk vs. reward, and so on. When the oncologist mentioned chemotherapy, it sounded like a teacher asking if he'd finished his homework. They make you feel like *no* is not an option. Unless…you're a coward, a quitter. Plus, you never knew, there were exceptions, percentages, even the all-elusive miracles. Mostly, chemotherapy was something he'd known would be part of the deal, no point in taking short cuts when it would all be over soon enough, anyway.

So, when that surgeon (why did they always look so healthy, anyway? Did they ever get sick? Were they even human?) asked him, at once a cliché and a formality, if his affairs were in order, he couldn't ascertain if he'd never been more eager for a reprieve from death, or ready for an imminent—and merciful—exodus from life. What his life had become. What he had done to his life.

Even then he knew. If he left his wife for a younger woman, it probably wouldn't work, no way it could end well. If he left the woman who loved him, he'd wind up alone, one day, dealing with some type of catastrophe. He also knew if he stayed, he'd never get sick and risk spending the entirety of his long, healthy, and predictable life wondering. Not quite fulfilled, still curious, still lacking…something.

And so, he'd been practical enough (or stupid enough) to understand: if you only get one go-round in this world, you're already playing with house money the minute you're born. What else is there to do but double down and dare fate to call your card?

That dalliance: it didn't really last long enough to call it a relationship, was over even faster than he would have imagined in the worst-case scenario. So fast he contemplated actually begging his wife, his *ex*-wife, to forgive him and take him back. But that wasn't going to happen, of course. That same loyalty he could have counted on, 'til death did they part, was now disgust. Or worse, ambivalence. At least his daughter merely despised him; his wife just…nada. Women can flip it like a circuit, all-in or nothing at all.

He's asleep again or wherever it is you go when you've pushed that button beside the bed enough times. You can never press that button too often, which is why they make sure your super juice is doled out judiciously, like a bunch of officious traffic cops eyeing the meter. His mother reached the point where she would get angry (Why isn't it working?) then pleading (Why do I have to wait so long?). He's noticed that every time he pushes it, it's working—they're not making him wait. That's good. But also not good; that means it's…bad.

His mother, in one of her last lucid moments, told him it was all almost worth it for the way the medicine made her feel. She explained, wide-eyed like a child seeing Santa Claus, that whatever they put inside those clear plastic bags, flowing like an ocean of serenity into her withered and bloodless veins, made her covet more time; anything just to experience that ecstasy as long as possible.

And he'd thought: maybe Huxley was onto something with his Soma: "All the benefits of Christianity and alcohol without their defects." Well, that's what he'd been searching for, with increasingly diminished returns, most of his life. Sure, whatever we consider reality would be bereft of authenticity, but if you could eradicate all earthly pains, who cares? It must be what a great white shark feels like every second of every day: just swimming, killing, sleeping. But does Jaws even know how good he's got it? Do we detect any arrogance in those impassive eyes? Do sharks have souls?

He's in confession, again.

A scared little boy, not smart enough to lie, too sensitive to see through the charade. What a sadistic ritual, making children feel ashamed at such a young age (if I should *die* before I wake?), and that's just for the things an 8 year-old can bring himself to admit.

And yet, was there not some value in having a semblance of self-control instilled, by any means necessary? Did it not set certain expectations that, even if no one else was watching (*He sees you when you're sleeping*), you were accountable for what you did? Did this convention deter some percentage of the psychopaths who might otherwise prey (*Let us pray!*) upon society? It would never be enough to eradicate all the atrocities, but if some less-than-secular mechanisms were put in place, total despair could perhaps be forestalled?

You had to hand it to Catholicism: they got to you early and often, and no matter how quickly—or successfully—you recovered from those formative scars, there was always the shame you could never shake.

Should he have eaten less red meat? Maybe. Avoided alcohol? Okay. Never placed a cell phone in his front pocket? Probably. Worked at a computer? Walked outdoors beneath a power line? Where does it end? How do we even know what causes cancer? Everything and anything, or nothing at all—just a dead end engineered into a faulty system. If not the Big C, it could have been a car accident, or a stroke, or a heart attack like the one that felled his father just after his fiftieth birthday.

Having cancer was unlike anything, other than just what it was: your body turning against you (against itself?). You couldn't hate your body (hate yourself?), but you could abhor the way it becomes a host for everything awful, a conduit for the thing trying to kill you. This was useful, because when regarded in its purest terms, you could isolate the pain and associate it with a proper cause. If not for this malignancy, this…invasion, your body would be *fine*.

Except it wouldn't be. Even by forty, his downward slope had been in full effect: sore knees, chronic neck pain, hangovers that lasted three days, the sudden concentration of unwanted weight in his mid-section. Way before those first symptoms, which he ignored until it was no longer possible, he had looked—and felt—increasingly less himself, the person he'd grown accustomed to being.

Okay, fine, he drank too much.

THIS KIND OF MAN

The longer, and harder, he continued hitting the bottles, set up in a seemingly ceaseless row, the more crucial it became that he'd quit smoking. Not necessarily for health-related reasons, but rather to become his ace in the hole, however unheroic. He could, at least, always look his primary care physician in the eye once a year, as they surveyed the mounting wreckage of unkept promises and unheeded warnings—the cholesterol count, those blood pressure numbers, the weird hairs sprouting like mutant weeds in the worst possible places—and confirm that he had not backslid on the cigarettes.

Not smoking? Shit, he now wished he'd gone full Marlboro Man. If something's going to get you, but you enjoy it, why not let it ride? Go all-in and never second guess yourself. Our bodies probably sense that caution anyway and punish us, accordingly.

What else? He could have read more. He should have. He could have watched some foreign films or tried harder to appreciate classical music. Or been a more adventurous eater. Travelled. But life's cumbersome enough, why give yourself homework? It's like the retired men and women he'd see jogging. What did they think, they were going to trick death? Did they hope they were changing anything? Sure, you can still fit into your wedding dress; enjoy that cottage cheese and skim milk. Great, same waist size as high school; you're like a sports car that sits in the garage, immaculate and immobile. Handicapping mortality was merely a different form of denial—doing everything except what you were designed to do.

Your mileage may vary. One of the most galling concessions he'd been obliged to make, after suppressing it (mostly successfully), was that he'd become a carbon copy of his father in all the worst ways. Metabolism of a hummingbird all through the first three decades, despite the staggering abuses during college, the sheer tonnage of shitty beer and processed foods, a fetid river of grease and saturated fat. Still, nothing; if anything, *too* thin. Then, his system turned on him like a mob informant, that cocksucker suddenly half-assing it like some government stiff watching the calendar until retirement.

But what was the alternative? Don't all these vegetarians and teetotalers feel the most cheated? Stretched out, at last, on the operating table, another slab of meat, however finely marbled, about to be butchered and, eventually, discarded.

He looks around and his sister is there. Yes, his eyes are open and it's her. This is bad. If she's there, this is it, it's over. No daughter? Either it's not *that* bad (yet) or she's on her way. Or she's not coming.

(He'd only stayed with his daughter once, back when there was some hope and enough time to…what? Make amends? Make up for lost time? No, just to have someone there, bound by blood if not love, to help him through the worst days—and nights—no one's ever fully prepared to face.

It made a difference, and while she never necessarily said her house wasn't an option going forward, it was his decision not to go back. He couldn't stand seeing his grandchildren afraid of him. He was, and for the entirety of their young lives had been, *Grandpa*, the one who tossed the ball, who went to their little league games, who took them out for ice cream. He was funny, he was fun, he was…Grandpa. That's how he needed them to remember him, not the half-monster in the

THIS KIND OF MAN

guest room, throwing up in a trash can or losing his balance in the bathroom.

It was excruciating, but in the end an easy call. He'd rather be alone and unmoored as opposed to ashamed, in front of those kids, on account of what his body was doing to him.)

His throat feels like a burlap sack. When he tries to speak it's like pulling that sack, in his mind, through a sink while the garbage disposal grinds away.

He sees the look his sister and the nurse give each other and feels the first rattle of real panic. He closes his eyes, just in time. His sister has never seen him cry, not even at their parents' funerals, or at his daughter's wedding, or during the phone calls, bringing her up to speed on the latest diagnoses.

Nobody but his father had ever seen him cry, and to remember that you'd have to go a long way back, back to childhood.

As an altar boy, he would occasionally be called on to serve a wedding and, less frequently, a funeral. Weddings of course were preferable: happy events, pretty women, typically a few dollars for his trouble. The funerals, obviously, were different in almost every way.

"Listen to the words," his father told him as he prepared for his first funeral mass. "It's actually a very beautiful service."

Incredibly, his old man was correct. The mass, while somber, also included much of the love and grace from the typical Sunday service, without the preachy or frightening parts.

It had been a sweltering August day and as he knelt, off to the side from the priest and assorted family and friends, he began perspiring through his heavy robe.

He leadeth me beside the still waters, He restoreth my soul...

Sweat mixed with tears as he experienced something he'd never associated with any church: something beyond awe, beyond peace, a sense that he was connected, in some way, to everyone in the world, all the people who'd come before and had yet to come.

He leadeth me in the paths of righteousness for His name's sake...

He woke up in the sacristy, his father smiling (his father never smiled) down at him. "You fainted," his old man said. Before he could respond, the priest bailed him out. "That happens all the time in the heat. It's even happened to me once or twice."

He cried and he allowed himself to cry (he was never allowed to cry), and his father took him for ice cream and told him he was a good altar boy, a good son.

Later in life, he could never recall the exact direction their conversation took, but it was most likely about sports, or the upcoming school year. It was, he knew, most definitely not about the funeral, or anything that happened in the church, and especially not the way he felt, or what he wanted to say but couldn't express.

No one was there. No wife. No daughter. No sister. No doctors. No nurses. No one. Nothing.

THIS KIND OF MAN

All right, let's review the record.

Best moments?

Marriage, first car, first house, first whatever, insert milestone here. Perhaps that one promotion? Not properly appreciated, because he was human. He foolishly counted on it being the first of many, each bigger, better, more significant. No clue that it would stand apart as the high point of a forgettable career; no idea that the pinnacle, such as it was, would occur with twenty plus years still ahead of him, two more decades of clock-punching and ass-kissing for...what? A paycheck, a purpose, a life. That's all? How could he have known? Nobody knows.

What about Bentley? Yes, his one and only dog, acquired post-divorce and pre-cancer. He loved that spoiled, lazy brute more than anyone, including his family, and that's something he'd take to the grave.

Bentley was a good dog, like all dogs are, but he was definitely a handful. That rascal would eat anything not locked away, or that he couldn't swipe out of your hands or off your plate. Shitting in the house with impunity, nothing to be done with him. In fairness, those early days were tough times, newly single with mornings where he slept through his alarm. How do you expect an eighty-pound dog to hold it in when you can't even leave the bed long enough to let him in the backyard?

He had a patience for that dog that he never possessed for his daughter and certainly none of his colleagues (extended family? Forget about it). He couldn't explain it and was too old to question it, but that dog made him want to be worthy of love. There were times when he looked at Bentley and saw, well, not himself, but his best self, the person he was, at his best, capable of being. Had he known this sooner, he would have made it a point to own dogs his entire life.

Bad moments?

There was that time at the company picnic: a drunken fist fight right on the softball field, in front of everyone. That embarrassment was regrettable, for all involved. Of course, it had happened during an extremely rough patch in his marriage. But still, you never quite recover from a spectacle like that, even if such things, in those days, seldom involved sit-downs with HR or, thankfully, immediate termination.

What else? The day he had to call his daughter, at college, and explain to her that he had moved out. And why.

Mostly, too many things he had said, or should have said, or never knew how to say.

Proudest moment?

Well…even after everything anyone could have predicted came to pass—older, alone, chronic illness—he resisted all urges to contact his ex-wife. He was, at least, man enough to avoid pulling her into the pathetic vortex of his final failure. At the end of a mostly decent, if unexceptional life, he figured, in the final analysis, he could take a modicum of pride in facing his pitiful end, alone.

Last confession?

Having processed everything else, he'd contemplated paying someone to cut his nails after it was over. A single idea tended to torture him: his toenails, still growing, crowding up against his newly shined wingtips, or his fingernails, stretching from his chest to his chin. But what were they going to do, dig him up? Delay the burial? Out of the question. Plus, if everything went according to plan, he wouldn't know or care about anything, anyway.

Wait! It's working, finally! I can feel it…I'm going to sleep!

No. Even in the darkness he can't turn it off; he's still at the mercy of the gray matter in his mind, corrupted before he ever had a chance.

He hadn't expected, much less hoped for any type of epiphany. Yet, there is clarity. He understands, at last, why so many people fight so hard to believe in *something*: it's the one commitment they could—and would—dedicate their lives to keeping. Even after diets, marriages, sobriety, fidelity; all those things almost everyone tries and fails, confronting the consequences of oblivion is…redemptory? Why hadn't he been able to fathom this? He doesn't know.

Yes, he does. It hadn't mattered to him until this moment because this moment had never actually occurred, until this moment.

He sees the light. Everyone is there.

All of them, including his daughter, even his ex-wife. And wait, how is his mother there, and the priest from that first funeral? Was his old man making his way through the crowd that somehow filled the room, spilling into the hallway?

He attempts to speak but he can't feel his face.

He reaches for the button, but he doesn't have hands.

He tries to close his eyes, but they're already shut.

He can still see them all, watching him, all deep in thought, or praying, or just…waiting.

COME AND GET MY GUN

"Do you know how fast you were going?"
Not fast enough, you don't reply.

You have somewhere to be, and you can't get there quickly enough. It's not your own bed (that's where you just came from) and it's not *her* bed (that's where you won't be coming again, anytime soon); it's the house you're usually driving away from at this hour, hoping to find the way home through half-shut eyes.

You've seen this little piggy before, you think, as he holds his flashlight expectantly in your face. And not just in those recurring nightmares where you manage to be the good guy *and* the bad guy; you recognize him and hope he doesn't recognize you. Maybe it's a blessing in disguise, you think, as he asks the question you never thought you'd want to hear.

"As a matter of fact, I have *not* been drinking," you say, so self-assured you start to second guess yourself, on principle.

Maybe you should bring him along—just in case—you think, as he takes your 411 to the squad car to make sure your references check out.

Maybe this is divine intervention, you think, forgetting for a second that it's been a long time since you remembered to believe in that kind of crap.

Maybe it's best to keep the law out of this, you know, signing on the thin black line. That's the last thing anyone needs: a man with a badge busting in on a desperate man with a gun.

***

There are certain elements that must fall into place in order for a mostly grown-up man to become friends with his best friend's father. First, the best friend needs to no longer be a best friend, or at least be out of the picture—say, in another part of the country. Second, his father must be recently widowed, or divorced, or otherwise apart from the best friend's mother. Third, and most important, your own folks must either be far away, or nothing at all like friends, or perhaps both.

Take a guy, like yourself for instance, and put him in a bar, alone on a work night, feeling sort of sorry for himself, and eventually he notices another guy, an older guy, also on his own, who has resorted to sweet-talking something on the rocks. That could be me, you think, and before you have a chance to follow *that* thought someplace you're not comfortable going, you realize: the reason he looks so familiar is because you know him. It's been several years since you've seen his son, but you used to know him like you knew yourself—in a neighborhood you came to outgrow the way you outgrew games, and bikes, and friends, and exchanged them for jobs, and cars, and co-workers.

THIS KIND OF MAN

Yes, that's him all right, the man who was an alternate father back in the day. Actually, he was always more like an uncle, letting you sneak those first sips at a time when there were only two types of beer: Heineken for special occasions; Budweiser for all the others.

"Buy you a drink?"

You don't mind if he does.

So, what brings you here, you don't need to ask.

Got nothing better to do, he doesn't bother to reply.

Instead, he talks about how his son has decided to stay out in California, because he realized he liked the seasons, so long as they were all summer.

"I know how you feel, sort of," you say. "My parents just joined every other retired couple down in Florida."

Then you joke about whether an earthquake will put his boy in the Pacific before the fulcrum of old folks breaks the southern tip into the Atlantic.

"I was gonna catch a cab," he says, after you've managed to toast some of the things you usually make it a point not to talk about.

"No, I can take you home," you say. You remember the way.

"So...what happened?" you say, after accepting the invitation to come inside for a nightcap and awkwardly hearing about the thing he couldn't tell you earlier.

"She's gone," he says, knowing it's not enough.

"Gone?"

"Well...she left. Six months ago."

You're not sure what's more uncomfortable: what he's just confessed, or how obvious it must be that you haven't spoken to his son in so long that you hadn't heard his wife was no longer a part of the picture.

"Can you believe it?" he asks, later, after a lot of other forgettable, forced things have been said.

As you reach for your keys, after respectfully being able to refuse one more for the road, you walk away convinced of two things, one worse than the other: you probably shouldn't come back; you know you're going to anyway.

Besides being your best friend's father, he was the only adult you were allowed to call by their first name. When you watch the re-runs in your memory filed under Childhood, he's a featured player, looming larger than teachers, coaches, and even those literary characters that are often among the best friends any sullen adolescent learns to find. Unlike your extremely careful, caring, and Catholic parents, he seldom seemed to say the word *no*: he always made popcorn during the ceaseless string of slumber parties, he took you to movies—back in the day when Rated PG actually signified something, he mixed up Shirley Temples with extra cherries and, later, virgin strawberry daiquiris—back in the day when saying the word *virgin* was more scandalous than the idea of a cocktail sans alcohol. Best of all, he was an unabashed smoker, which meant that stolen cigarettes—back in the day when sneaking menthols was cool (back in the day when people smoked menthols, for

THIS KIND OF MAN

that matter)—comprised a crucial part of your coming-of-underage.

So: you begin going over once a week. He hasn't lost his touch in the kitchen—the same touch you never found—and he masterminds meals just like he had a thousand other nights all through the '80s. You eat, you listen to old blues albums, you watch movies, you embellish adventures from the good old days, and try to avoid any mention of the bad new days. Most of all, you drink. He makes a mean martini; he makes a nice martini too. He knows his wine, he knows his single malts, he even has beer from countries that haven't discovered electricity. Always obligatory cigars and cognac before last call; the host slumped over in his leather chair, snifter safely empty in lap, scorned Cuban smoldering in ashtray.

Like the unsullied early stages of any relationship, you enjoy the rush, eventually settling into a routine. Predictable and mostly pleasant, until the night he pulls a gun on you.

"So..." he says, slurring, not that anyone's noticing. "How come you haven't sold your soul so far?"

"You mean marriage? Well..." you recognize the stale response, as it happens to be the truth. "I guess I just haven't found the perfect person yet."

He snorts and nods his head.

"You're smarter than most people; too many young men need to make a mistake before they figure out how happy they actually were."

"Are you happy now?"

You both look around the room to see who the idiot is who just asked that question.

"Never been happy," he says, then quickly adds: "Never been *happier* I mean."

You both laugh, but it only helps a little. Good time for a bathroom break. You take your not-so-sweet time, and when you return there's a gun on the table where his beer used to be.

"How come you haven't asked me what happened?"

Because I don't want to know, you don't say, unsteadily finding your seat.

But your silence won't suffice. So:

"Another man?"

"Even worse than that."

"Another *woman*?"

"Nothing."

"Excuse me?"

"Nothing! She'd rather be on her own than be with me."

Silence.

"Do you have any idea what that's like?"

More silence, which seems better than any other options you can come up with.

"I'll tell you this," he says, uncomfortable with the silence (it's mutual), or with where his imagination is invariably going, or both. "If there *was* another man, I'd shoot him, you know…if he ever came around here."

He picks up the gun—a snub nose? Colt 45? Revolver? Whatever it is, it looks a lot like the ones in those movies you

THIS KIND OF MAN

like to watch where fake people pump fake bullets into fake bodies forming pools of fake blood.

"I never thought I could kill a man, unless maybe they were breaking into my house, which is why I have *this*," he holds the gun up, menacing an intruder who isn't in the room.

He stands up unsteadily (To get more beers? To put on more music? To go to the bathroom? To go to bed?) and does the one thing you hoped wouldn't happen: he tightens his grip, stabbing the air as he speaks.

"Do you know what it feels like to look in the mirror and know that everything you ever worried about is coming true? You're old, you're ugly, you're angry, and you're alone."

I never think about those things, you can't say. To yourself.

Everyone made it out alive, and here you are, another week, another dinner, another drink, another inexorable lull in the conversation where someone might slip up and say something substantial.

"There's something I want to show you," he says, standing up.

Oh no, your eyes say.

"Out in the garage," he smiles, leading the way.

"Here it is...the real reason my wife left me," he adds, apparently without irony.

"What number is this?"

"The fourth. So, including my son, I've had five babies." Again, no apparent irony.

SEAN MURPHY

He Who Dies With The Most Toys Wins, the bumper sticker says.

The first Porsche was not a mid-life crisis, unless it's possible to have a mid-life crisis at thirty-two. Of course, our fathers formed a generation that did everything early, either because they figured it out faster or learned the truth too late: married before twenty-five; kids before thirty; second mortgage for college tuition by thirty-five; quiet desperation in full effect by forty.

"Wanna see what she's made of?"

"Hell yeah. Next time I'm over let's take her for a whirl."

"Next time? Why not right now?"

"Do you know how fast you were going?"

He hands his license over, smilingly to the cop, and shrugs his shoulders, neither defiant nor necessarily contrite.

"Sorry about that officer…just blowing off some steam."

"Doing seventy-five? You do know what the speed limit is on this road, don't you?"

"Probably a lot less?" he tries.

"Probably reckless," the officer answers.

"Damn, I didn't even know this thing could go that fast!"

The officer is not amused.

"Actually, there's troubles at home," he says, switching gears more artfully than you could ever have imagined. "Taking a little ride with my son here. My wife left…"

THIS KIND OF MAN

And then two miracles occur: the officer doesn't ask if you've been drinking and he lets everyone off without so much as a warning.

After the valedictory cocktail, still too nervous to drive, you opt for crashing on the couch instead of into a tree. It's a sleepover full circle from the '80s.

Is this the way it works? You don't ask as the room spins into sleepiness. Of course, they can arrest the kids, they *should*; they have to. But it doesn't make anyone feel good to haul in a man old enough to know better. Or maybe it's just dumb luck. Fate, as only the truly unlucky understand, waits until you're on the ropes, then moves in with ever-humbling haymakers. Perhaps even Fate wouldn't stoop *this* low; pouring ketchup on a man with a lot to lose, while he's bleeding.

Morning. Your host is already dressed and brewing coffee before you can get off his couch.

"Need a Bloody Mary?" he calls from the kitchen.

The only response more irresponsible than this offer itself would be to refuse it.

"Shit. I need to stop drinking," he announces. "It's just as simple as that."

"Me too," you say. "Want to give it a shot?"

"Actually, I put in two shots," he says, handing you the drink. Without irony, you think.

More of a man than you, he's on his way to work while you're on your way to your own couch. No way of earning a dishonest day's pay, not today: you'll pay your dues in equal installments of sweat and regret.

You still have hangovers, thank God.

Everyone who has known an alcoholic knows that as soon as you stop feeling the pain, you're no longer feeling much of anything.

Everyone can think of a friend whose father (or mother for that matter) was in an entirely different league when it came to the science of cirrhosis. The man who falls asleep fully clothed, then up and out the door before sunrise, like the rest of the inverted vampires who do their dirty work during the day in three-piece suits. Maybe it's a martini at lunch, or several cigarettes per hour to take the edge of. Whatever it is, whatever it takes, they always make it out, and they always come back, to the family and the refrigerator, filled with the best friends anyone can afford.

Our fathers came of age in the bad old days that fight it out, for posterity, in the pages of books, uneasy memories and the wishful thinking of TV reruns: the '50s. Men who have *rye* in their liquor cabinets—who still have liquor cabinets for that matter. These are men raised by men who never considered church or sick-days optional, and the only thing they disliked more than strangers was their neighbors. Men who didn't believe in diseases and didn't drink to escape so much as to remind themselves exactly what they never had a chance to become. Theirs was an alcoholism that didn't involve happy hours and karaoke contests; theirs was a sit down with the radio and a whiskey sour, a refill with dinner and one before, during, and after the ballgame. Or maybe they'd mow the lawn to liven

THIS KIND OF MAN

things up, tinker under the hood of a car that had a long way to go before it could become a classic. Or perhaps, friends would come over to play cards. Sometimes a second bottle would get broken out. A slow burn of similar nights: stiff upper lips, the sun setting on boys playing baseball, mothers sitting on the couch watching TVs not yet paid off, forced smiles battling bottled tears in the bottom of a coffee mug, amphetamines and affairs, evening papers and a creeping conviction that there is no God, of poets unable to make art out of the mess they'd made of their lives.

It was a hard time where people didn't live happily ever after, if they ever lived at all. It was a time, in other words, not unlike our own.

Take a guy, like yourself for instance, and put him in a bar, alone on a work night, feeling sort of sorry for himself. Naturally, he notices the good-looking girl across the bar looking at him. And the reason she looks so familiar is because you know her, in many senses of the word. And before you can figure out what to think about this—what to *think*—she's on her way over.

"Buy you a drink?"

You don't mind if she does.

"So...what brings you here?" you ask.

"Looking for someone."

"I guess you knew where to find him?"

It wasn't that hard, she doesn't need to say.

So…what happened?

You find yourself alone again, on your way home, away from a warm bed and a warmer body that most likely won't be welcoming you inside anytime soon.

"That's so *sweet*," she'd said, after you explained how you'd come to befriend your best friend's father.

"Well, it was fun while it lasted," you started to say.

"So…what happened?"

And you told her the story: dinners, movies, drinks, and the day divorce papers were filed. The day he decided, once and for all, to dry out.

"I got the call," (you said), "and showed up fully supplied: steaks, a bottle of France's finest and Italy's most expensive, even some champagne, in case it turned into that kind of evening, in case we needed to toast something."

"And?"

"And he said: *It's over.*"

"I know," (you'd said). "That's why I broke out the heavy artillery."

"No. It's *over*. I'm done. No more martinis, no more vino, no more hangovers, no more nothing."

"Well, that's wonderful!" (she said).

I guess so (you thought). "But, well, when we weren't drinking, everything was different. I tried, but the dinners were just…different. *He* was different."

"Well, what did you expect?"

THIS KIND OF MAN

"I don't know. Just, suddenly there wasn't anything to talk about. Or there was *too* much to talk about. Every time I thought of something to say, it seemed like the wrong thing. He didn't want to talk about her; I didn't want to talk about *you*...we ended up talking about nothing."

"So...what happened?"

"What do you expect? It all got too uncomfortable, I just sort of stopped going over."

"That's terrible."

"You're telling me! That was a free meal once a week."

"That's not funny."

"No, really. I mean this guy *knew* his wines, and where else am I gonna score authentic Cubans?"

"You're pathetic."

"Well, what did he expect? What was I supposed to do, be his goddamn shrink?"

"You were supposed to be his friend."

"Look at it this way," (you said), after you'd attempted to say several things, each of them increasingly ineffective and ill-received. "If I'd been *there* tonight, I wouldn't have been at the bar to see you!"

So: what happened?

She went looking for the guy she thought she remembered.

And what was the problem?

She found him.

Phone ringing.

"Hey, it's me…"

A blast from the past—a voice from back in the day when saying *it's me* meant you knew exactly who it was.

It's your former best friend, sounding like what he is: someone you haven't heard from in a long time; like someone's son.

"Listen, I'm worried about him," (he calls his father by his first name, just like you always did, back in the day).

"He called me," he says.

He called me too, you don't say.

"And he said some stuff that really upset me, and that's why I'm calling you…"

You don't say anything.

"He called me *your* name," he says, after he's gone on to say some other things, some of them familiar, some of them shocking, and some of them more than a little incriminating. "And before he hung up, he said: *Come and get my gun.*"

***

So: the cop lets you go, without a warning and with a ticket, a little something to remember him by. And you think: What am I going to do? What am I going to see? What am I supposed to *say*?

He doesn't say anything: after you've knocked, rang the bell, and eventually let yourself in. There he is (sobbing), there's

THIS KIND OF MAN

the gun (waiting), there's a mess: bits of bottles everywhere. In the sink and on the floor, a small fortune of broken spirits, dying angry deaths in the open air. He has destroyed all the things that could hurt him, the new enemies he could no longer resist the old-fashioned way.

And so: should you be appalled, or at least embarrassed? Unprepared, you remember the backyard baseball games, crying during a scary TV show, or pissing your pants, and all the forgotten things you did because you didn't know any better. And this man, always there, because it was his job. The man who could have been your father, now old enough to be a grandfather. This man who needs someone who is not there, so now it's your job.

You look around: nothing cooking in the kitchen, no movies on, or music in the background, no beers in the refrigerator—there is nothing left, including excuses. You take a deep breath, and then say in a voice very unlike your own:

Talk to me.

ACKNOWLEDGMENTS

Before I wrote my first (terrible) poems, I wrote my first (terrible) short stories. I'm happy to name names and thank John Taliaferro, my fifth-grade teacher, who not only tolerated, but encouraged these efforts, and also introduced my class to the discipline and joy of journal writing, a habit that took and has stayed with me through the decades. I was subsequently blessed with several instructors who provided similar feedback and motivation, without which perhaps I would have put down my pencil and picked up a remote control. A first draft of one of the stories in this collection was written for a fiction workshop class in 1991 (!) and I salute Stephen Goodwin (himself a wonderful author) for telling me to start sending to start sending my stories out to literary journals. Outside the classroom, of course, is where the real learning (and magic) occurs, and I can't begin to thank—or list—the artists who have guided and galvanized me.

Of course, before teachers and touchstones, I had the fundamental gift every writer requires: parents. Eternal gratitude to Jack and Linda Murphy for providing more than enough support and encouragement; without you none of this would be possible, on literal or artistic levels. Thanks to Janine for being my big sister, marrying Scott, and raising two of my favorite people, Madeleine and Anthony. If there are too many friends to list (there are) special thanks to Mark Seferian and David Greenspan—the Apha, Omega, and Everything in Between. I offer my deepest esteem to Morgan Ryan, Kim Churches, Ben Mayrides, Tom Hoyler, Jeff Coker, Mark Hanlon, A.J. Hernandez, Justen Ahren, Jim Boyer, Tony James and, of course, Foolene & the Slush Man. Chuck Cascio and Devon Hodges will always hold an special place in my Irish heart. We all need miracles, and the nourishment I receive from Ace, Shieldsy, Jamey, Chet, and Matt is a miracle, repeated daily. Ardent blessings to the team at Unsolicited Press for believing in my work. A more exhaustive accounting of my debts is offered in the back of previous books, so seek them out and support some arts non-profits while you're at it.

Obviously if, as a writer, one finds words insufficient, that's either the worst or best thing. Heather Murphy, thank you for being the best thing, proving to me that loneliness is neither necessary nor advantageous for creative types. Thank you for expanding my very conception of what love can be; the family we have—including not only Ben and Ellie, but Bootsie and Benson—exceeds any fantasies about adulthood and fulfillment I may have once entertained.

A final thought. All one need to do is read the news to find ample evidence of intolerance, mendacity, greed, and ill-will—and despair, accordingly. But engaging with the world, working and living amongst human beings who have been hurt, who struggle, who can't catch that break, who'd love nothing more than an opportunity to thrive, obliges one to judge warily, and find ways to cultivate empathy, even for the inexplicable. As such, while some of the characters in this book are drawn in part from people I've met and things I've heard or seen, they've all been creatively concentrated through the filter of fiction, and are intended not to answer questions but oblige them. Can even the most misspent life offer lessons? If we refuse to make the same mistakes, doesn't this defiance signify a sort of progress? If we grudgingly acknowledge the loss of those who couldn't—or wouldn't—be helped, might we cultivate our indignity to prevent further injustice? Can new connections be established? Can more dialogue be initiated? Can a debate begin? Can our world be saved, one exchange at a time?

ABOUT THE AUTHOR

Sean Murphy is founder of the non-profit 1455 Lit Arts, and directs the Story Center at Shenandoah University. He has appeared on *NPR's* "All Things Considered" and been quoted in *USA Today, The New York Times, The Huffington Post,* and *AdAge.* A long-time columnist for *PopMatters,* his work has also appeared in *Salon, The Village Voice, Washington City Paper, The Good Men Project, Sequestrum, Blue Mountain Review,* and others. His chapbook, *The Blackened Blues,* was published by Finishing Line Press in 2021. His second collection of poems, *Rhapsodies in Blue* was published by Kelsay Books in 2023. His third collection, *Kinds of Blue,* and *This Kind of Man,* his first collection of short fiction, are forthcoming in 2024. He has been nominated four times for the Pushcart Prize, twice for Best of Net, and his book *Please Talk about Me When I'm Gone* was the winner of *Memoir Magazine's* 2022 Memoir Prize. To learn more, and read his published short fiction, poetry, and criticism, please visit seanmurphy.net/ and @bullmurph.

ABOUT THE PRESS

Unsolicited Press is based out of Portland, Oregon and focuses on the works of the unsung and underrepresented. As a womxn-owned, all-volunteer small publisher that doesn't worry about profits as much as championing exceptional literature, we have the privilege of partnering with authors skirting the fringes of the lit world. We've worked with emerging and award-winning authors such as Shann Ray, Amy Shimshon-Santo, Brook Bhagat, Kris Amos, and John W. Bateman.

Learn more at unsolicitedpress.com. Find us on twitter and instagram.

www.ingramcontent.com/pod-product-compliance
Lightning Source LLC
LaVergne TN
LVHW040045080526
838202LV00045B/3497